RENEGADE LAWMAN

Gordon D. Shirreffs

Rowan Emmett, ex-marshal of Silver
Rock, had spent ten years in prison on a
false charge. Now he'd come back to kill
the men who'd put him there. Cassie
Whitlow, the town madam, was his only
friend, and she knew better than he did
the odds against him. She knew it would
take more than a fast gun to keep him
alive long enough to find his
vengeance . . .

RENEGADE LAWMAN

Gordon D. Shirreffs

Curley Publishing, Inc.
South Yarmouth, Ma.

Library of Congress Cataloging-in-Publication Data

Shirreffs, Gordon D.
  Renegade lawman / Gordon D. Shirreffs.
    p. cm.
  1. Large type books. I. Title.
[PS3569.H562R4 1990]
813'.54—dc20
ISBN 0–7927–0282–4 (lg. print)   89–28799
ISBN 0–7927–0283–2 (pbk. : lg. print)   CIP

Published in Large Print by arrangement with Donald
MacCampbell, Inc. in the United States, Canada, the U.K.
and British Commonwealth.

Distributed in Great Britain, Ireland and the
Commonwealth by CHIVERS LIBRARY SERVICES
LIMITED, Bath BA1 3HB, England.

Printed in Great Britain

RENEGADE LAWMAN

CHAPTER ONE

Something long familiar was missing as Rowan Emmett rode his roan up the eastern side of the ridge that separated Silver Rock from the desert. He drew rein on top of the ridge before he realized what it was — the low thunder of the stamping mills was gone. Rowan cupped a light to his cigarette. "There she is, Smoky," he said to the roan. "Silver Rock. Once the mining capital of Arizona Territory. Silver and blood. Faro and roulette. Gunsmoke and lead. Red lights and tinny pianos." He spat as he finished the bitter comment. Ten years had made its mark on Silver Rock. Ten years in Yuma Pen had certainly made marks on Rowan Emmett's body and soul.

The mining town, sprawled over the mesquite-studded slopes of the Grindstone Hills, was an irregular group of adobes, jacales, warped wooden buildings and rusted mining structures, gaunt against the late afternoon sky. Long shadows had crept down into the town, and here and there the sharp rectangular shapes of lighted windows showed against the oncoming night. Rowan scratched

1

the salty crescent beneath his right armpit. "We need food and a bath, Smoky," he said with a grin. "Leastways, *I* need a bath." He touched the roan lightly with his spurs and rode down toward the town.

Silver Rock *had* changed, Rowan noted as the roan jogged easily past the outlying buildings. Streets that had once bustled with miners, tinhorns, shady ladies, vaqueros and gunslingers now seemed deserted. An occasional figure could be seen here and there, hurrying as though the shadows held too many memories. There were no lights up at the mine. Stores were boarded up. Here and there some of the flimsy, jerrybuilt structures had collapsed. Rowan was almost in the center of town before he saw a few stores that still showed signs of activity. The Territorial Bar was lit up. *That* at least hadn't died with the rest of the town.

Rowan swung down from Smoky and tethered the roan to the saloon hitching rack. He slapped the dust from his clothing with his battered hat, eased his gunbelt and touched the smooth walnut of the Colt butt. He had paid for his crime at Yuma Pen, but there might be those who hadn't forgotten Mike Ganoe, Larry Farber and 50,000 dollars in silver bullion. Rowan pushed through the batwings and studied the

2

men in the bar quickly through slitted gray eyes.

There were only half a dozen men in the big saloon, three of them playing cards. A drunk sagged in a chair tilted against the wall. A man was absorbed in his newspaper. There was but one man at the high bar. Rowan scratched his lean jaw. In the old days it would have been a quiet night at the Territorial if there were less than fifty customers. He walked to the end of the bar. The soft jingle of his spurs caused everyone but the drunk to eye him momentarily before they returned to what they had been doing.

The bartender got up from his high stool and shuffled down toward Rowan, stifling a yawn. "Evenin'," he said, "your pleasure." Suddenly he placed his hands flat on the bar. "Rowan Emmett!" he said softly. "Well, I'll be damned!"

Rowan smiled. "Hello, Andy," he said. "It's been a long time. How's the beer?"

"Fine. Just fine, Rowan." Andy drew a beer and shoved a platter of cheese and crackers before Rowan. "How long you been out?"

"Couple of months. Worked down in Sonora for a while."

Andy's washed-out eyes avoided Rowan's searching gaze. He took a cigar from the case

3

and gave it to Rowan. "Fresh in last week. A good smoke. How long you stayin'?"

Rowan sipped his beer. "Hard to say."

"Just passin' through, eh?"

Rowan shrugged. "Why? You worried, Andy?"

Andy waved a fat hand. "Not about *me*, Rowan. About *you*. Some of the people here in Silver Rock ain't forgot what you did." The barkeep shuffled off as the man at the end of the bar banged down his glass for service. When Andy reached him the man leaned across the bar and spoke quickly, eying Rowan. Andy nodded hastily and filled the glass.

Rowan helped himself to the free lunch. There had been a time when Rowan Emmett had been liked and trusted in Silver Rock. As deputy marshal of the town he had often acted as bullion guard, escorting shipments to the railhead. After six months of that duty he had been asked to ride shotgun with Mike Ganoe on the bullion wagon. Larry Farber – a mine guard and Rowan's best friend – had gone along. They had decided to take the ingots out at night on the little-used Creek Road. There had been a hell of shooting a few miles from town. Old Mike had pitched silently from the driver's box. Rowan had turned to see where Larry was. It was then the slug had struck alongside Rowan's head, coursed along the skull and had tumbled him into an abyss of pure darkness. Rowan shoved back his hat and traced the scarred line of the bullet's path along the side of his head. He still got hellish headaches from the wound.

Andy came back to Rowan. "Ain't much doing in the way of mining here any more. Mines flooded two years ago. The company tried everything. Water kept comin' in. There's still a lot of silver under this town, though."

Rowan drained his glass. "Anyone ever find Larry Farber?" he asked quietly.

"No . . . Seems an odd question for *you* to ask, Rowan."

"So Silver Rock still thinks I did him in?"

Andy spread out his hands. "That's what the jury decided, Rowan. It wasn't never my personal opinion, you understand," he added hastily. He went to refill the beer glass.

Rowan closed his eyes. When he had come to after being knocked out he had looked up into angry faces of some of the townspeople and mine officials. It was dawn. Mike Ganoe still lay in the rutted road, staring at the graying sky with sightless eyes. Rowan was pulled to his feet. The canvas wagon cover had been slit from end to end. The wagon was empty. Larry Farber's horse grazed near

5

the road, the saddle bloody. That had been the beginning of a nightmare for Rowan.

Rowan could still mentally reconstruct his days in the *calabozo*, his trial and sentencing, and then the long journey to Yuma Pen. He had been accused of killing Larry and caching the fifty thousand. Prosecutor Trevor Paine had painstakingly dug up evidence that Mike Ganoe had once been mixed up in a bullion theft in Sonora. The damning thing had been that Mike had been killed by a .44 slug. Rowan carried a .44 Colt and .44 Winchester whose cartridges were interchangeable. Two shots had been fired from the Winchester. Rowan's story that Mike had been killed at the first gunfire had been disproved, for there was one empty hull in Mike's Colt. Larry's sidearm had been a .41 Colt Lightning and his saddlegun a 45/70 carbine. Paine's skillful story, woven tightly, had been that Mike and Rowan had planned the whole deal. Larry had been done away with and the bullion hidden. Then Rowan and Mike had fallen out. In the ensuing gunplay Rowan had killed Mike and had himself been felled by a slug from Mike's Colt. The trail, greased by Trevor Paine's slick tongue, had skidded Rowan straight into the hellhole of Yuma.

Rowan shoved the free lunch back. Thinking of the trial had cost him his

6

appetite. Paine had been so damned slick. There had been no tracks apparent, other than those of the wagon team and Larry's horse, anywhere near the scene of the crime. No one had ever found the silver.

The batwings swung open and a tall man came in, blinking in the light. He glanced at Rowan and then came forward, holding out his hand. "Rowan Emmett! Good to see you!" It was Archer Lang, who had been a mine employee at the time of Rowan's residence in Silver Rock. Rowan gripped Lang's hand. "Glad to see you, Arch," he said.

"Andy!" called Archer. He gripped Rowan by the shoulders. "It's been a long time. How was it?"

Rowan spat. "Frozen in winter, roasted in summer."

"Anyway, it's all over."

Rowan tilted his head. "My sentence is. Andy tells me Silver Rock hasn't forgotten me."

Archer lit a cigar. "Count *me* out of that. I was always on your side, Rowan. You know that."

"I guess I was a fool to come back."

Archer glanced at Rowan over the flare of his match as he lit his cigar. "Why *did* you come back?"

"Sheer cussedness. I still want to clear myself."

"You've served your time. Let it rest. Believe me, it's the best way."

Rowan slowly shook his head. "I'll be damned if it is. Larry was my best friend. Mike Ganoe was shot to death as he sat beside me. Fifty thousand in silver is missing. Do you think I can let that rest?"

"Then take my advice – walk quietly and keep your hands off your guns. There are still friends of Larry's here in town. There are others who think you know where the silver is. You've paid your debt to society, but *they* won't agree to that. Do you have a place to stay?"

"Not yet."

"I've got the best room at the hotel. Two beds. Tell the clerk you're moving in with me."

Rowan gripped Archer's shoulder. "Thanks, Arch, I'll pay you back somehow. I'm going to get this trail dust off."

He left the bar. The streets were dimly lit by lights from windows. A man was leaning against a post at the end of the saloon porch. When he saw Rowan untether Smoky he flipped away his cigarette and strode off into the darkness.

Rowan left the roan at the livery stable and

entered the hotel. He placed his saddlebags on the floor in front of the counter in the lobby. The clerk looked up. "Can I help you?" he asked.

"Archer Lang said I could share his room."

"Good." The clerk turned the register toward Rowan and handed him the pen. Rowan wrote his name quickly. The clerk turned the register again and read the name. He looked up at Rowan. "I'm sorry," he said quietly. "You can't stay here."

"Why not?"

The clerk flushed. "This is a respectable place, Mr. Emmett."

Rowan placed big hands flat on the counter. "Does Amos Darby still own it?"

"Yes. Why?"

Rowan grinned crookedly. "He's getting mighty fussy, isn't he?"

"I don't understand."

"Amos got run out of Tombstone for running a crooked faro game. He was also mixed up in the Chacon smuggling ring down in Sonora for a few years until the Rurales chased him north of the border. He's got a helluva nerve keeping *me* out of his hotel."

The clerk raised himself to his full height. "You can't stay here!"

Rowan leaned across the counter, gripped the clerk's coat front with one hand and then

9

rounded the counter. He shoved the little man hard against the wall. "Give me the key," he said thinly, "or I'll make a neat impression of the back of your head in the plaster. Savvy?"

The clerk reached for the key and gave it to Rowan. Rowan shoved the clerk back. "I spent ten years in hell for a crime I didn't commit," he said over his shoulder as he started up the stairs. "I've paid my way."

A man who had been reading a newspaper in a far corner of the lobby watched Rowan go up the stairs. His heavy eyelids dropped over his dark eyes. He raised the newspaper until Rowan reached the top of the stairs and then he came over to the desk. "That was Rowan Emmett, wasn't it?" he asked.

"Yes, Mr. Sharpe."

Walt Sharpe nodded. He glanced up the stairs and then left the hotel.

Rowan nodded in appreciation as he entered Archer's big room. Three windows looked down on Bonanza Street, while three on the Second-Street side of the hotel afforded a view of the dark ridge and hills east of the town. Two big beds stood side by side. A comfortable easy chair stood beside a marble-topped table littered with cards, newspapers, a half-empty bottle of rye and several glasses. Rowan opened the closet door and ran his hand down half a dozen fine suits, nodding

10

his head in appreciation. Another door opened into a bathroom. "Some class," he murmured as he stripped off his trail-worn clothing.

Bathed and refreshed, Rowan lit a cigar and filled a glass with rye. One of the newspapers caught his eye. It was dated a month previously, and one item was encircled with pencil. *Rowan Emmett was released from Yuma Prison early last month*, he read. *Emmett may be remembered by old-timers at Silver Rock as the man who was convicted of the murder of Michael Ganoe in a bullion robbery ten years ago. Not one trace has been found to date of the body of Lawrence Farber, another of the ore guards, nor of the fifty thousand in bullion which disappeared the night of the robbery.* Rowan drained his glass and turned away.

He dressed slowly, putting on his wrinkled black suit, white shirt and Mex boots. He drew his Colt, checked the loads, then slipped it under his waistband. There was forty dollars in his wallet; he wouldn't last long on that. He was about to leave the room when someone tapped on the door. "Come in!" he called.

The door swung open and Walt Sharpe came in. "Hello, Rowan," he said. He extended a soft hand.

Rowan gripped the hand without enthusiasm. "How are you, Walt?"

Walt looked about. "High tone," he said.

11

"But then, everything about Arch Lang is high tone."

"So? What's he doing now?"

"Mostly gambling. Speculates. Invests. Anything with the taint of big money about it."

"Like you."

Walt's heavy-lidded eyes studied Rowan. "Yes," he said softly, "like me."

Rowan jerked a thumb. "Drink?"

"Don't mind if I do."

Rowan filled two glasses and handed one to Walt. "Regards," he said and downed his drink swiftly. Sharpe had always been friendly enough to Rowan, but Rowan had never liked him.

Walt walked over to a front window and looked down into Bonanza Street. "You staying long in town?"

"Depends. Why?"

"I guess you know why."

"Yes."

Sharpe rubbed his plump jowls. "I've still got a lot of pull here in Silver Rock, Rowan."

"So?"

Sharpe turned. "Did you come back for the bullion?"

"In a way."

"What do you mean?"

"I came back to clear myself. If the silver is

12

still cached hereabouts I'll try to find it."

Sharpe laughed. "Everyone in town has dug at least one hole looking for it. What makes you think you can find it?" He came closer to Rowan. "Or do you *know* where it is?"

Rowan refilled his glass. "You're poking your nose in deep, aren't you, Sharpe?"

"Maybe. Look – I'll make a deal. If you know where it is, I'll help you get it out of town for a fifty per cent split. I can do it, Rowan."

"I'll bet you can," Rowan said dryly.

"Is it a deal?"

"No."

Sharpe flushed. "I can make it damned hot for you if you don't come across."

"In the first place, I don't know where it is. In the second place, even if I did, I wouldn't throw in with you, Sharpe."

Sharpe stepped back. "A lot of honest citizens weren't satisfied when you got away with a ten-year sentence, Rowan."

Rowan grinned. "Honest citizens? Diogenes would have gone loco trying to find one here in Silver Rock when I left. Or has it changed that much?"

"I've got a lot of friends who agree with me."

"Friends? You mean hired gunslingers, don't you?"

13

"Does it matter? You know what I mean."

Rowan turned and opened the door. "Get out," he said, "before I plant a boot against that fat rump of yours."

Sharpe sidled past Rowan. "Don't you try nothing now," he warned, glancing up the dimly lit hallway.

Rowan looked up the hall. "Who's down there?"

"No one."

"You're a damned liar! I never saw you go anywhere without a bodyguard, Sharpe. You're safe, if that's what's worrying you."

Sharpe licked his lips. "Just don't you go and throw in with anyone else, Emmett. I got here first. I'm a big man in Silver Rock. Another thing: You keep your mouth shut about me being here. Understand?"

Rowan laughed. "I wouldn't want to spoil my social standing by admitting it. *Vamonos!*"

Rowan closed the door and walked to the front windows. Sharpe left the hotel. A moment later, a man wearing a black Mex hat, heavily ornamented with coin silver, and a light-colored buckskin jacket, took a post in the doorway of a vacant store across the street from the hotel. Rowan shrugged. He took a double-barreled derringer from one of his saddlebags and hung the bags over the back of a chair. He slipped it into his coat pocket

14

and left the room. He paused long enough in the lobby to light a smoke and then left the hotel, ignoring the scowling clerk.

Buckskin Jacket was still in his doorway when Rowan set off for the western edge of town, walking swiftly, as though on an errand. Past empty stores, ramshackle houses and weed-grown lots until he stood at the bottom of Boot Hill, somber in the windy darkness. He walked up the path until he found Mike Ganoe's sunken grave. The weathered headboard was aslant. Rowan cupped a lucifer against the wind and read the inscription. *Mike Ganoe. 1815-1878. Murdered by a bullion thief. Our loss is Heaven's gain.* He blew out the match.

As Rowan reached the bottom of the hill something, or someone, moved in the shadow of an old shed across the street. Rowan walked back toward the center of town. When he had left Silver Rock this end had been called Crib Row, the place of business for the cheaper-priced shady ladies. Now the shacks were dark and sagging. He could remember when they had been aglow with lights and noisy with the sound of drunken laughter. He wondered where the inmates were now.

Rowan cut off at Fourth Street and walked up the sloping street toward the mine buildings. He glanced back. The street was

15

deserted. Suddenly he stumbled forward, lost his balance and slid partway down a slope, gripping a rock that protruded from the loose earth. Earth and stones slid past him with a soft rush and pattered on a hard surface far below. He crawled back up the slope and lit a match. A wide hole stretched in front of him. It reached from one side of the street to the other and was fifty feet across. He knew then what it was. A collapsed stope. The streets must be undermined with many old drifts. He shuddered a little. He might have cracked his skull far below and remained there for days until he was found. Hell of a note, not having a barricade erected there. It showed how far Silver Rock had come since the old days.

Rowan walked slowly back to Bonanza and headed for the Territorial. He glanced up at Archer's room as he passed the hotel. The lights were out. He paused, not remembering as to whether he had put them out or not. He shrugged and continued on toward the bar. There was always a fire hazard in those boom towns, composed mainly as they were of sun-dried wood. They were touchy as tinder. He wondered if the old volunteer fire department was still in existence. Atlas Number One, it had been called. He grinned as he thought of the red shirt, trimmed with double rows of mother-of-pearl buttons, which he had worn

16

as an honored member. They had had good times at the firehouse socials, even if their fire-fighting record had not been the best.

CHAPTER TWO

The thick tobacco smoke hung in rifted layers throughout the Territorial Bar when Rowan entered. There were several games going under the yellow light of low-slung harp lamps. A lean man, dried from the suns of Arizona, sat in the high lookout stool. His eyes flicked toward Rowan and then down at the closest game. Yet Rowan felt that the man hadn't dismissed him at all. Rowan saw Archer Lang seated at a table in the corner, riffling a deck of cards through his slim hands, evidently waiting to start a game. Rowan got a bottle and two glasses and sat down beside Archer. The gambler smiled. "You look different," he said.

"I feel different. Nice room you've got, Arch."

Arch waved a deprecating hand. "Best I can get. Silver Rock doesn't offer much any more. Not since the City House burned to the ground five years ago."

17

"Silver Rock *has* changed. I took a walk after cleaning up."

Archer's eyes lifted. "Where?"

"Up to Boot Hill. Saw Mike's grave."

Archer nodded. "See anyone else?"

Rowan filled the glasses. "Walt Sharpe dropped by. I practically booted him out of the room."

The cards slipped easily through Archer's hands. "What did he want?"

"You know damned well what he wanted! He thinks I know where the bullion is hidden. Offered me a deal. Protection and a split if I took him to it."

"So? I had an idea you'd be damned popular hereabouts. In that respect anyway."

The batwings eased open and Buckskin Jacket came in as silently as the draft of air that followed him. He stopped at the bar and raised his head to look into the mirror behind the bar, quickly eying Rowan, and then he ordered a drink. Archer glanced at the newcomer and then at Rowan. Rowan leaned closer to his friend. "Who is he?"

"Goes by the handle of Durango. They say he was a scout against the Apaches. I say he lived with them."

"Gunman?"

"Knifeman."

"Works for Walt Sharpe, I'd imagine."

Archer nodded. "Been tailing you?"

"Yes."

Archer downed his drink and lit a slim cigar. "Watch him."

"Troublemaker?"

"No. Works in the dark. Like a damned weasel."

Rowan studied the man when he had a chance. His face was laced with a network of fine sun-wrinkles. His black mustache was neatly trimmed and waxed. His eyes were in almost violent contrast to the darkness of his face; they were a light, almost whitish blue. A stag-butted Colt hung at his left side, butt forward for a cross-arm draw. The tip of a sheathed knife showed below the right hip of his fancy buckskin jacket.

Walt Sharpe came into the bar, passed behind Durango, muttered a few words and then sat down at a table near the rear. He looked at Archer. "Game tonight, Arch?"

"If you like," said Archer.

Sharpe's veiled eyes studied Rowan. "How about you, Emmett?"

Rowan shook his head. "I'm short," he said.

Archer felt beneath his black coat. "I'll stake you, Rowan."

"No." Rowan refilled the glasses. "I want to look about a bit."

"Be careful."

Rowan grinned. "I'm not worried," he said quietly. "So long as Silver Rock still thinks I know where the bullion is, I'm safe enough."

Archer smiled. "The same old Rowan."

Rowan glanced at his friend. "What have you been doing since Silver Rock went on the skids? Doesn't seem like your kind of town any more. You always went where the big money was."

"There is still plenty money hereabouts. Cattlemen, miners from the hills and merchants."

"After Dodge City, Hays and Deadwood, Silver Rock must be damned dull to you."

Archer looked up from the cards. "I've a reason for staying."

"So? What is it?"

"Ellen Farber is here, Rowan."

The name struck Rowan like a thrown knife. He had thought a lot of Ellen, and particularly during the long nights at Yuma. He had courted her in the old days but had bowed out when he had realized Larry Farber had the inside track. "What's she doing?"

"Works for Jim Bond at the newspaper."

Rowan stood up. "I'll be getting on. I'll drop by later."

Archer nodded. "Cassie Whitlow is still in town, too." He looked up at Rowan.

20

Rowan rubbed his jaw. "Can't figure it out. You and Cassie still in town. Cassie always followed the big money."

"She was gone for a while. Came back some months ago and opened a small place over on Mesquite Street. Calls it Cassie's Castle. Drop by and see her."

Rowan waved a hand. Walt Sharpe came forward as Rowan turned toward the door. "Don't forget what I said, Emmett," he said quietly.

Rowan tilted his head to one side. "You play your games with Archer," he said. "I'm through playing with tinhorns."

Sharpe shrugged. "All right. All right. But walk careful, Emmett. Silver Rock hasn't forgotten you."

"I haven't forgotten Silver Rock." Rowan headed for the door. The lean man in the lookout seat was watching him. His eyes dropped as he saw Rowan glance at him. Rowan stepped out into the street. It was lit by the moon, lending a gentle touch to the drab buildings. Rowan rolled a smoke and walked slowly toward Mesquite Street. At the corner he stopped and stepped into a doorway. A moment later Durango appeared, looked uncertainly up and down Bonanza Street and then hurried off in the opposite direction. Rowan grinned. An imp spoke

21

into his ear. Rowan crossed Bonanza, ran down to Yucca, and turned to follow the street, paralleling Durango's course. He cut up Second Street, glancing up at the hotel. A man passed along Bonanza. It was Durango. Rowan followed him all the way to Fourth and then stepped into the deserted street. He grated his boots on the hard earth and then eased back into an old stable that was but a shell of its former self. It was dark in the stable. The old smells rose about Rowan as he stepped behind a rough-hewn upright. Boots scraped the earth outside the stable and Durango stopped in front of the stable, looking up and down the street.

Rowan moved forward swiftly. He hooked an arm about Durango's neck, clamped a hand on his right wrist and hauled him back. Suddenly Durango arched his back, driving his rump into Rowan's belly, breaking the hold. Durango whirled in time to meet a jolting right to the jaw. He went down into deep shadow and came up like an uncoiling spring in time to meet Rowan's right boot. The heel caught him under the chin and his jaws snapped together. He grunted in pain and anger.

Rowan caught a swift movement. He threw himself sideways as the knife shot past his head. It struck a post and quivered there.

22

Rowan closed in, gave Durango the boot once more and stepped back to look down at the unconscious man. With a hard grin Rowan knelt beside him. He ripped the jacket up the back from bottom to collar. He took out the stag-butted Colt and emptied it, throwing the gun into the stall beside Durango. He looked about for the fancy black Mexican hat and carefully trod on it, grinding his heel in hard. He pulled the knife from the post and cut Durango's gun belt and trouser belt. He threw the knife up against the roof of the stable, where it struck hard. Rowan dusted his hands and left the stable, heading up Pitahaya Street toward Mesquite. He rolled a smoke, whistling *Billy Venero* as he strolled along. He felt good for the first time since entering Silver Rock.

Cassie's Castle, read the sign, fresher than most Rowan had seen in the town. It was lettered across the front of a rock building that stood at the corner of Mesquite and Pitahaya. The windows were shuttered, but the cracks were bright with yellow light. Half a dozen hip-shot ponies were tethered at the rack in front of the place. A man lay face down in the gutter, snoring off a drunk. Rowan opened the door of the saloon and stepped in. A girl was picking out a tune on a once ornate piano. Her bright red dress was a splash of vivid color against the faded finish of the piano. Two other girls, one in yellow, the other in a vivid green dress, stood at the bar, laughing with two cowpokes. Rowan looked about. It wasn't bad, but compared to Cassie's old place up on Bonanza it was just a hole in the wall.

The bartender looked at Rowan. "Your pleasure, sir?"

"Cassie about?"

"Who wants to know?"

"Tell her Rowan Emmett is here."

The barkeep nodded and walked to the end of the bar, opened a door and disappeared. A moment later he came back. "She'll see you," he said. He eyed Rowan closely as he walked to the door.

Rowan entered a passageway. A woman giggled from a room at the end of the hall. A door was ajar. Rowan tapped on it. "Cassie?" he called.

"Don't be so damned formal, Rowan. Come in."

Cassie Whitlow sat behind a littered desk. Her hair was still golden, held together at the nape of the neck with a clasp, allowing a pair of thick curls to drape across the full breasts that were half revealed by the black sheath gown she wore. Her brown eyes held Rowan's. She held out a slim hand, and

24

Rowan took it. She was still a fine-looking woman, although she must be damned close to forty by now. "Sit down, Rowan," she said. She filled a glass for him from a cutglass decanter. The light from a shaded lamp flattered her. Rowan felt some of his old interest in her revive. Cassie and he had been pretty close years ago.

Cassie leaned back and took a cigarette from a silver box. "The prodigal returns," she said in her husky voice. "You're crazier than I am, Rowan."

Rowan leaned back and loosened his coat. "I never expected to see you here, Cassie."

She drained her glass and laughed shortly. "Times are changing in Arizona. Cassie Whitlow! Once the toast of the boom towns, now the queen of half a dozen girls, catering to drunken cowpokes and sneaky merchants hiding out from their wives." There was intense bitterness in her voice.

Rowan studied her. Now that his eyes were used to the light he could see the change in her. Her once fresh complexion was covered heavily with make-up. Her eyes were tired. Her hair must have been tinted, for it was too golden. Ten years had made a difference in the Golden Girl. Rowan had a quick mental picture of her riding in a barouche drawn by fine black horses. Three other girls with her, riding down Bonanza Street to buck the tiger at one of the fancy dives.

"Why did you come back?" he asked.

"Maybe I was waiting for you."

Rowan smiled. "Not *you*, Cassie. I never had enough money to have *you* chase me. What chance did I have with men like Walt Sharpe, Amos Darby and others?"

She studied the liquid in her glass. "You were a *real* man, Rowan. Mean as a rattler sometimes, gentle as a lamb at others. There were times when you and I were almost like sweethearts and there were other times when we hated the sight of each other." She looked up at him and drained her glass. "It was fun though, wasn't it?"

"Yes. But why did you come back?"

"The mines may be pumped out."

"Perhaps. You intend to wait that long?"

"I've got a good little business here. I've got enough to take care of my old age."

"You'll never get old, Cassie."

She laughed. "You sound like a courting lover. Look at me, Rowan Emmett!" Her voice showed signs of the liquor she had been drinking. "Tell me I'm the same woman who was the toast of Silver Rock years ago."

Rowan smiled. "We all age, Cassie. You're a damned good sport. Take it as it comes."

26

"Damned good sport!" she hiccuped. "Tell me you love me! Tell me you'll die for me! Go on!"

Rowan refilled his glass and tried to ignore her as she thrust hers forward. She gripped his wrist, and he filled the glass. "You're drinking too much, Cassie."

"Who wouldn't around here? I used to have the best bloods in town coming to my place. Men who were as much at home in the best places in New York as they were in my place. Men with fortunes at their disposal. Gentlemen, mind you! Now all we get here are drunken cowpokes, smelling of manure, dust and sweat, pawing you with hands as hard as boards."

Rowan leaned back in his chair. "Take it easy. You can always leave."

Her face grew hard. "No. I'm staying."

"But why, if you hate it so?"

She looked away. "I've got reasons."

"Not a man?"

"Maybe." She looked at him. "You were a fool to come back, Rowan. Most of the people here still think you know where that bullion is hidden."

Rowan shook his head. "I've come to clear myself, Cassie."

"You served your time. Get out of here. Go get a ranch. Marry some country girl. Raise

27

a family. Use your head. *Get out of Silver Rock!*"

"I'm staying."

She shrugged. "I might have known you would." She eyed him closely. "You broke?"

"I'm not flush," Rowan admitted.

She opened a drawer and placed a thick roll of bills on the desk. "How much do you need?"

"I don't want anything."

She shoved it toward him. "Listen – I'm loaning it to you. Pay me back when you can. I've never forgotten you, Rowan."

"Arch Lang is letting me stay in his room. I can get money from him if I need it."

For a fraction of a second there was a strange light in her tired eyes, and then she smiled. "Take the money. More than once you helped me keep my place from getting shot up when you were marshal. You saved me thousands then. The least I can do is help you now."

Rowan took the bills and stowed them away. "You'll get it back soon, Cassie." He stood up. "I've got to see Archer now." She followed him to the door and placed her back against it, looking up at him. The heavy odor of her perfume drifted about him. She looked up at him. "Is thanks *all* I get?"

He slipped an arm about her waist and

28

drew her close. Her lips met his. She clung to him with a passion that surprised him. She placed her head against his chest. "Be careful, Rowan."

"Why?"

"You've paid enough. You don't know how many times I cried, thinking of you at Yuma."

Rowan kissed her. He opened the door. She leaned against the wall. "Sometimes I wish we could go back and do things all over again. What changes we could make."

"I wonder. Perhaps we'd do the same things all over again."

She held him with her eyes. "I don't think so."

They walked into the barroom. "Hey, Cassie!" a man yelled, "Flora wants me to marry her!" He clung to the girl dressed in green. Cassie forced a smile. "Go ahead. You'll both be back here in a week. Cadging drinks."

Rowan walked to the door and turned. "I'll see you soon, Cassie."

She nodded. "Ellen Farber works at the newspaper. Or did you know?"

"Yes."

"I suppose you'll be seeing a lot of her?"

"No. How can I, after being accused of killing Larry?"

Cassie came close. "I don't think she ever believed it."

"Still, there'd be a lot of talk if we became friendly."

She squeezed his wrists. "Don't make any mistakes, Rowan. You always loved her. She's young and lonely. Do as I say. Get out of town. Take her with you."

"Cassie, you're drunk."

"Certainly I am! Do you think I'd tell you that if I wasn't?" Cassie turned. "Amy, dammit! Play that piano! Let's get some life in this hole! See you later, Rowan."

Rowan stopped outside to roll a smoke. The odor of her perfume clung to him a little. Even the tobacco seemed to hold it as he lit the cigarette. He flipped it away and headed toward Bonanza Street. Ellen Farber. He wondered if she would go with him. Cassie Whitlow knew people. He wondered if she knew Ellen that well.

Rowan entered the Territorial. Archer Lang sat at his table, dealing cards to Walt Sharpe and two other men. Rowan hooked a chair and turned it, dropping into it and resting his arms on the back. Archer nodded at him. "Drink?" he asked.

As Rowan shook his head, a man came through the batwings. It was Durango. He had on a buckskin jacket, but it wasn't the same one he had been wearing earlier that evening. His jaw was swollen. His hard eyes bored into Rowan's, and Rowan looked away, trying to stifle a grin. The man leaned against the bar and watched the card players. Rowan yawned. "Guess I'll go to bed," he said. "Long ride today."

Walt Sharpe looked up as Rowan stood up. "I'm buying," he said.

"No thanks." Rowan sauntered past Durango, so close he almost brushed the man. Durango shot a look of pure hate at him. There was an itchy feeling between Rowan's shoulder blades as he left the saloon and headed for the hotel.

He unlocked the room door and lit the lamp. The room looked almost the same, but something had been changed. He looked at his saddlebags. They were still hanging over the back of the chair but they had been reversed, because he had taken his derringer from the right-hand bag and left it unbuckled. The left-hand bag had been buckled and had been hanging over the back of the chair. Now it was the right-hand bag that was over the back of the chair. He walked to his dusty trail clothing, lying in a heap near the bathroom door. He could have sworn they had been arranged differently when he had left. What did you expect? he asked himself

31

as he undressed for bed. He put out the lamp and slipped his Colt under his pillow. He was safe as long as everyone believed he knew where the bullion was cached.

CHAPTER THREE

Rowan got up early and dressed quickly, moving quietly so as not to awaken Arch Lang, who had come in long after midnight. He left the hotel and breathed deep of the fresh desert air. The sun was just rising over the hills, but the coolness of the night still clung about the town. Rowan walked quickly to the nearest restaurant and sat down at the counter. He was reading yesterday's newspaper, waiting for his food, when something made him turn as the door opened. A woman stood there, waiting for a man who was talking to another man on the sidewalk. Rowan stared at her. There was no doubt that it was Ellen Farber. Ten years had changed her, too, but the change had deepened her attractiveness. She must be about twenty-eight, or twenty-nine, Rowan reckoned, for she had been about five years younger than he when he had been sentenced.

Rowan's breakfast was placed before him, but he could not take his eyes from Ellen. She stood watching the two men outside, but her profile was in full view. The same tip-tilted nose and calm gray eyes, the soft brown hair and softer mouth. Her simple dress set off her figure to advantage. Rowan stood up and walked up behind her. "Hello, Ellen," he said.

She turned quickly. Her eyes scanned his face as though expecting to see a man broken by ten years in a man-made hell. "Rowan Emmett," she said quietly. "I heard you were in town."

"I was coming by to see you," he said.

"I'm glad. Jim wanted to talk with you."

"Jim?"

"Jim Bond, my employer."

Rowan nodded. He glanced at the shorter of the two men outside. He hardly remembered Jim Bond, an Easterner who had bought the newspaper shortly before Rowan had left Silver Rock. As Rowan looked at him, Bond turned and came into the restaurant. He glanced quickly at Rowan. "This is Rowan Emmett, Jim," said Ellen. "He just got back yesterday."

Bond thrust out his hand. He was short and well built, with just a trace of thickening girth. His brown eyes were frank and friendly.

"Have breakfast with us," he said. "I've wanted to talk with you." He led the way to a table, and the waitress brought over Rowan's meal. "Go ahead," said Ellen. "Don't wait for us."

Bond leaned forward. "How long do you intend to stay in Silver Rock, Mr. Emmett?"

"Call me Rowan. I don't know."

"Somehow I never believed you were guilty, Rowan."

"You hardly knew me then, Jim."

Bond waved a hand. "Ellen has worked with me for some time. We've often talked about you."

Rowan looked at Ellen. A faint flush mantled her cheeks. "I always thought you were innocent, Rowan."

Rowan smiled. "First people in Silver Rock to say that. It's almost worth the trip here from Sonora."

Bond rubbed his smooth-shaven face. "I'll say you've got nerve coming back here."

"I've already been reminded several times that I'm not too popular."

Bond sipped his coffee. "I'd like to hear the whole story ... from *your* viewpoint. The old files of the paper don't tell much except Trevor Paine's point of view."

Rowan shoved back his plate. He took out a cigar and looked at Ellen. She nodded. Rowan

34

lit the cigar and leaned back. "We had fifty thousand in silver bullion. Ingots. Left the mine office at nine P.M. and rode out on the Creek Road. Two miles from town we dipped down into Sandy Wash. There was a shot. Mike Ganoe was hit in the back of the head. I turned to shoot and was hit by a slug." Rowan traced the line of scar alongside his head. "When I came to, it seemed as though half the town was out there. It was dawn, and the wagon was empty. Larry's horse was grazing south of the road, blood on the saddle. You know the rest."

"I never could understand why you left that late at night, on a road that was hardly ever used."

Rowan puffed at his cigar. "There had been some talk of bullion thieves. We passed the word around that we were leaving the next morning on the usual road. Someone knew our actual time of departure and the route."

"Seems odd that fifty thousand would be entrusted to three men."

Rowan nodded. "I agree, except for the fact that Larry and I worked well together and Old Mike was a good man with a gun. We figured the fewer men who were in on the deal the less talk there'd be. Maybe Larry and I were *too* sure of ourselves. In fact, we were."

Bond finished his food. "You haven't given

me much to think about. Isn't there anything you can add to the story so that we can do some work on it?"

"Have you ever seen Yuma Prison, Jim?"

"No."

"The main cell block has thirty-four cells built like ovens, running clear through the building. They're narrow and high with arched ceilings. In the middle of this tunnel is an iron grating, and at each end a grated door. In each of these two sections are six hanging bunks with hardly enough room for a man to swing his legs over the side to get down to the floor.

"Each night the doors were locked after we were chained to ringbolts in the floor. I had a top bunk. From dusk until dawn, sometimes, I would look up at the ceiling and go back over what happened on the Creek Road, minute by minute. I'd go back over each minute of the trial, trying to find a clue. Anything that would give me the answer to why an innocent man had to spend ten years in hell for something he didn't do." Rowan shook his head. "I never found the answer."

Ellen looked away. Jim Bond glanced at her. "Then you think you'll find the answer here?"

Rowan leaned forward and gripped the newspaperman by the arm. "Yes! *Someone* must know! Somewhere here in Silver Rock I'll find a shred of evidence and I'll unravel this whole mess."

"I hope you do. I'll help you, but it seems as though the deck is stacked against you. First – Mike Ganoe was found dead. Second – neither Larry Farber nor his body has ever been found. Third – fifty thousand dollars in bullion is still missing."

Rowan nodded. "Yes. *It's still missing.* Unless the man, or men, who did the job managed to get it away, it must still be hidden near Silver Rock. I'll stake my life on that. People think I've come back for it. Good! Someone will talk."

"What then?" asked Ellen quietly.

Rowan looked quickly at her. "I'll give him the same chance Larry and Mike got."

"That won't help you, Rowan."

Rowan stood up. "Perhaps not. But they won't catch me this time."

Jim Bond looked at Ellen. "Open the office, Ellen. Perhaps Rowan would like to walk you there. I've got a few things to do before I write this week's editorial."

Later, in the street, Rowan looked down at Ellen. Her face was set. "You want me to turn the other cheek. Is that it?"

"No. Jim and I will help you all we can,

and if you do solve this mystery you must see that the culprits are brought to justice. It's not for you to judge them, Rowan."

"Why do you say *culprits* and *them?*"

"I could have just as easily said *culprit* and *him*, Rowan."

"But you didn't."

She stopped and faced him. "What's wrong with you? You're so bitter, so suspicious. Do you think I know any more about this terrible crime than you do?"

"No."

"Then let me alone. I've suffered enough these past ten years. Losing Larry and thinking of you in that filthy prison."

"You never wrote, Ellen."

She turned and walked on, stopping at the office. She unlocked the door and went in, hanging up her hat and shawl. She sat down at her desk and looked up at him. "What did you expect?" she asked. "The widow of the man you were accused of killing couldn't write to you without causing talk."

"You weren't always in Silver Rock."

She flushed. "I never expected to see you again, Rowan."

"I'm here now. Does it make a difference?"

"I don't know what you mean."

He smiled. "We'll see. Good morning, Ellen."

Rowan stepped out into the street. Two women were watching the office from across the street. They turned quickly and walked off, glancing back over their shoulders. There'll be plenty to talk about at tea today, thought Rowan. He walked slowly up Bonanza. Men eyed him from behind store windows or from doorways. Wondering. Here was a man thought to have killed two men for fifty thousand in silver bullion. Fifty thousand that had never been found. Rowan grinned wryly as he relit his cigar. He had brought new life to dying Silver Rock.

A man was standing on the boardwalk in front of Bengson's General Store as Rowan approached. Rowan stiffened a little as he recognized the lean hawk face, the arched nose and the hollow, piercing eyes. It was Trevor Paine, whose eloquence had sent Rowan to Yuma. The lawyer adjusted the cuff of his left sleeve. Rowan stopped in the street and looked up at Paine. "Hello, Paine," he said quietly.

The slim white hand fiddled with the cuff. "How are you, Emmett?" asked Paine.

"Well enough for a man who lost ten years of his life."

Paine glanced up and down the street. "The trial was just, was it not?"

Rowan shrugged. "Evidently. You won in any case."

"What do you mean?"

"Nothing. You had the odds. You've lost few cases, Paine. May you always win."

"I'm not sure that I like your tone."

Rowan flipped away his cigar and came closer. "I don't want you to. Now ... you can stop playing with that cuff. You won't need the stingy gun hidden in there. Your time hasn't come yet."

Trevor Paine flushed and dropped his hands by his sides. "You're like a dog in the manger," he said, "snapping and growling at everyone. Be careful, Emmett. You felt the hand of the law once. It can reach you again."

Rowan stepped back and bowed. "Administered by the honorable Prosecutor Trevor Paine."

"I'm no jailbird at any rate!"

For a moment white-hot hate swept through Rowan. His right hand tensed, as though to reach for his Colt, and then reason got the better of him. "Stick around, Mr. Paine," he said softly, "There may be other jailbirds roosting in Silver Rock." He turned and strode off. He heard Paine's low, mocking laughter as he entered the livery stable to see how Smoky was getting on.

The roan whinnied as Rowan came in.

Rowan rubbed Smoky's neck. Smoky was the one sure friend he had in Silver Rock. Hell of a note when a man's *only* friend was a horse. Rowan left the livery, calling out to the liveryman, "I'll need him this afternoon!"

Rowan entered the Territorial Bar. The place had the sour morning smell of stale tobacco smoke, liquor fumes, dirty water and sweat. The swamper was mopping under the tables. Rowan stepped up to the bar and the swamper soused his mop viciously in the bucket. "Damned whisky hounds," he growled. "Can't even wait until the place is clean."

Rowan turned quickly. He eyed the old man. As the swamper walked behind the bar, the hobbling gait seemed familiar. The gray beard was ragged and stained with tobacco juice. A pair of eyes, amazingly bright in so wrinkled and damaged a face, peered at Rowan past a beak of a nose. "I'll be damned!" said Rowan. "Hardtack Christie!"

"Who the hell are you?" grumbled the old man. He stared at Rowan. "Rowan Emmett! I'll be double-damned!" He gripped Rowan's hand with a claw. "You make a break? I'll hide you, son. I ain't forgot you."

Rowan shook his head. "I served my time. I'm free, Hardtack."

Hardtack poured two stiff hookers. "Seems

like yesterday since they railroaded you down the river, Rowan." He shoved the glasses toward Rowan and hooked an elbow over the edge of the bar. "Drink up. There's more where that came from."

Rowan sipped his drink. "What the hell are you doing swamping in here?"

Hardtack rolled his eyes upward, downed his drink, cleared his throat and looked at Rowan. "Mother's milk. I been working here about a year, Rowan."

"No more prospecting, eh? What'd you do with all your money?"

Hardtack poured another drink. "Now you won't believe this, Rowan, but there was a nice little filly down to Globe who took a liking to Old Hardtack. We had quite a time, me and Angie. Lost my pile there."

"You ought to be ashamed of yourself."

Hardtack bowed his head. "I am. I'm a miserable old reprobate."

"Cleaned you out, eh?"

"In a way. I made another strike years later and headed for Tucson to spend it. Guess what happened the first night I was there?"

"Angie?"

"So help me. Have another drink."

Rowan grinned at the old man. Hardtack Christie had braved Apaches to penetrate into the Grindstone Hills and find the float that had been the indication that he was standing on a veritable hill of silver. He had started the rush that had made Silver Rock a town of six thousand people a month after silver was discovered. He had sold his claim for one hundred thousand dollars and later saw the same claim sell for three times that much. Since that time, the ore output of the mine had soared skyward, making millionaires out of the men who ended up with Hardtack's claim.

"You remember the old days, Rowan?" The old man licked his thin lips. "Me, Horatio Christie, riding around town in a barouche drawn by matched blacks. Me, Horatio Christie, wearing a top hat, checkered vest and the finest suit west of the Mississippi! Me, Horatio Christie, throwing gold pieces on the floor of every bordello in town and smacking the hurdy-gurdy girls on their plump little rumps with my goldheaded cane as they scrambled for 'em."

Rowan shook his head. "You were a misguided boy, Hardtack. A callow youth of fifty-five led astray by too much money and liquor."

Hardtack fixed Rowan with a keen eye. "Seems to me you helped me thin down my bankroll more'n once, *amigo*."

"That I did."

Hardtack waved an expansive, dirty hand. "No matter. I lived. Those were the days, Rowan."

"I never expected to see you swamping, Hardtack."

"It's a living. Damn it! Meals and a bed. Thirty bucks a month and what I sweep up with my broom. Never sweep up much. All tinhorns nowadays, Rowan. Why, I remember dropping a gold piece on the floor now and then to help the swamper along. These tinhorns today would pick up a damned penny they dropped."

Rowan studied the old man. He was a living legend. No one knew how many thousands he had been worth at his peak. His body was scarred with bullet and arrow wounds. He knew every trail and canyon for hundreds of miles as he knew the palms of his dirty hands. Some men said he had spent more time underground than most miners had spent above ground. Old Hardtack *was* Silver Rock.

Hardtack emptied his glass. "Why'd you come back?" he asked.

"Figured I'd grubstake you, Hardtack."

"Hawww! I couldn't find a piece of float no more."

"Maybe you could find fifty thousand in silver bullion."

The old man placed his glass carefully on

the bar. His face had paled. "Now why the hell did you have to bring *that* up?"

"You know why."

Hardtack wiped his mouth. "Yeah. Yeah. Guess I do." He shuffled back to his mop and bucket, jerked out the mop and began to mop the floor with great energy.

"What's eating you, Hardtack?"

Hardtack leaned on his mop. "Why not forget the whole thing, Rowan?"

"You know me better than that."

The old man nodded in resignation. "Yeah. Yeah. Mebbe you don't know it, but there's a whole passel of hombres hereabouts been waiting for you to show up. Damned if you don't do it, too. Supposing you *do* find the bullion. You think you'd get it outta here?"

Rowan clapped a hard hand down on the bar. "I don't intend to. I want to clear myself."

"Yeah. Yeah. Of the stealin'. How about Mike and Larry? You think finding the silver will clear you of *that?*"

Before Rowan could answer, a man pushed through the batwings. It was Amos Darby, owner of the hotel. He had always reminded Rowan of a fat fish, slightly bloated with some kind of disease peculiar to the finny tribe. His suspicious green eyes flicked from Rowan to

45

Hardtack and back again. "Hello, Emmett," he said in his colorless voice.

Rowan nodded. Darby stroked his plump chin. "I heard you were in town, staying at my hotel."

"Your clerk wasn't anxious to have me register, Amos."

Darby waved a fat hand. "I spoke to him about that. You've served your time. He had no call to do that."

"Thanks, Amos."

Darby glanced at Hardtack. "You and Hardtack been talking about old times?"

"Yes."

Darby cleared his throat. "Come on back to my office. I own this place now. Like to talk with you."

"Later, Amos. I've got some things to do."

"As you wish." Darby walked to the rear of the saloon and turned. "If there is anything I can do to help you, let me know. Always like to help old friends." He entered a hall, and a moment later a door closed farther down it.

"Amen," said Hardtack, casting his eyes upward.

Rowan threw some coins on the bar. "See you later, Hardtack," he said.

Hardtack glanced at the rear of the saloon. "Yeah. Yeah. We'll talk about old times, Rowan. You get it? *Old times.*"

CHAPTER FOUR

Rowan walked up First Street toward the hills that rose behind Silver Rock. The rusted mine structures stood out boldly in the clear air. There was an odor of decay about the once busy area. He passed shacks whose windows were boarded. Here and there he saw hollows where the earth was sinking in on the drifts that honeycombed the ground beneath the hills and slopes. Rusted and broken pieces of equipment littered the ground. Broken glass had been tinted pink and blue by the desert sun. It was deathly quiet. Rowan wandered about the area, once humming with activity and the shouts of the mine employees. He sat down on a rock and looked down at the town. Dust rose from beneath wagons' wheels on the main road. Winding off to the east was the rutted trace of the Creek Road. He could almost make out the arroyo where the holdup had taken place.

Rowan lit a cigar and sat there for a long time, mulling over his experiences since returning to Silver Rock. He had angered Walt Sharpe and Trevor Paine, and he was sure Durango knew who had waylaid

47

him. There was an undercurrent of fear in some of those he had spoken with. Archer Lang had warned him to walk quietly. Walt Sharpe was sure Rowan knew where the silver was. Cassie Whitlow had warned him to get out of town. Someone had gone through his effects. Perhaps Ellen Farber knew more than she would speak of. Trevor Paine would not forget Rowan's remarks. Amos Darby had offered friendship, but Rowan would as soon accept the friendship of a *bronco* Apache. Hardtack Christie was afraid of *something*.

A man rounded the corner of First and Bonanza and started the long climb up the street toward the mine. It was Archer Lang. Archer came slowly up the hill and sat down beside Rowan, fanning himself with his large white hat. "You still rise early," he observed.

"Used to get up at dawn in Yuma, Arch."

Archer lit a cigar. "What are you doing up here?"

"Thinking."

Archer glanced about at the rusted machinery. "Nice place to think. Seems strange that thousands in silver is still somewhere beneath us, doesn't it?"

Rowan looked quickly at his friend. "What do you mean?"

"I mean the silver ore that was never taken out. The flooded parts of the mine probably contain more silver than was ever removed. Water was struck at five hundred feet and rose quickly. Engineers think a subterranean river or lake was tapped." Archer inspected his cigar. "Odd thing is that the drifts under the town never flooded. Maybe it saved the town."

Rowan spat. "For what?"

Archer leaned back and crossed a leg. The sun glinted on the fine polished leather of his out-thrust boot. "Damned if I know. What do you plan to do next, Rowan?"

"Ride out on the Creek Road."

"What do you expect to find there? That area has been covered with a fine-tooth comb."

"I've got to start somewhere."

Archer nodded. "I suppose. Did you have a run-in with Durango last night?"

"Yes. why?"

"My God, Rowan! Why did you antagonize *that* man?"

Rowan grinned. "I don't like being followed. Is he sure it was me?"

Archer shrugged. "A friend of mine told me Durango was talking with Walt Sharpe late last night. He overheard Durango threaten to kill you, as he was sure you were the one who ambushed him. It was bad enough knocking him out; by ripping up his clothes you made a fool of him – and what's worse, a personal enemy."

Rowan stood up. "It's a habit I acquired at Yuma. You either fight back there or go through hell from the other prisoners. I'm going back to town to get my horse."

"I've got nothing to do until tonight. Can I come along?"

Rowan smiled. "I meant to ask you."

Later they rode out on the Creek Road. It had never been used much in the old days, and from its condition it looked as though it had never been used since then. Rowan drew rein in the arroyo where the attack had taken place. There the wagon had stood. There was the place where Larry's horse had been found. Rowan swung down and walked about. Archer sat his black and watched him. It was getting hot, and a slow trickle of sweat worked down Rowan's sides as he looked about. He passed through a clump of mesquite and around the base of a knoll. The arroyo cut south, running deep into the eastern slopes of the hills. Rowan climbed partway up the knoll and studied the terrain. He could see the mine structures plainly to his right. Which way had the thieves taken the silver? He shook his head at the hopelessness of it all and walked back to Archer.

Archer hooked a slim leg about the pommel

of his saddle. "Learn anything?" he asked.

"No."

"Someone else is trying to learn something."

"What do you mean?"

Archer lit a cigar. "Don't look right now, but on that mesquite-covered slope half a mile from here someone is using field glasses. I caught a flash from them."

Rowan bent down to look at one of Smoky's hoofs and then glanced toward the slope. There was a minute flash of something, as though the sun was reflecting from a polished surface. "I see what you mean," he said.

"You can expect things like that wherever you go."

Rowan swung up on Smoky. "Someone looked through my saddlebags and clothing up in your room last night," he said.

"Naturally."

"What should I do, Arch?"

"You can either leave here or stick it out. If you leave you'll only have to come back secretly to look around. It wouldn't be easy. Someone would see you."

"And if I stick it out?"

"I'll help you. I can get things done if you trust me."

"You know I do."

Archer smiled. "I've done a lot of thinking

about that missing silver, Rowan. It isn't likely it was brought back into town. It isn't easy to secretly convey fifty thousand dollars' worth of silver. Someone would likely have seen that going on, yet there never has been the slightest indication that someone *did* see it."

"So?"

"Isn't it possible that the bullion was hidden out here somewhere?"

"Yes. In fact I'm sure it was. For a time, anyway."

"What do you mean?"

Rowan glanced up at the slope where the hidden observer had been. There was no sign of him now. "I think whoever engineered the job hid the bullion out here, waited until things blew over and then hauled it out."

Archer shook his head. "You know how stories and rumors float about this country. There never has been the slightest inkling that the bullion was cashed in anywhere in the Southwest. There never has been any indication that Larry Farber didn't die the time the bullion was stolen."

"What do you mean by that?"

Archer relit his cigar. "Did it ever occur to you that Larry's disappearance was damned mysterious? Mike was left dead in the road. Evidently the killer, or killers, thought you were dead, too, or they would have made sure after shooting you off the wagon. But why did they hide Larry's body? Why Larry alone, when they left two other men bleeding in the road?"

Rowan was puzzled. He glanced at Archer. The gambler's face was impassive. "Larry might have escaped and been shot down later. He might have been seriously wounded, and crawled off to die."

Archer shook his head. "No. The buzzards would have located his body for the law. The ground between here and town is pitted with holes dug by men looking for the bullion. They've covered every inch of the ground. They would surely have found Larry's body."

Rowan rubbed his jaw. They were nearing the town now. Several loungers watched them covertly as they passed the first buildings. "I'm not sure what you're driving at, Arch," he said. "But speak out with it. Just what *are* you driving at?"

"Maybe Larry was mixed up in the robbery."

Rowan turned quickly. "Damn you! You've gone too far, Arch!"

Arch smiled. "Take it easy, Rowan. I'm only trying to help."

"Larry was my best friend. We'd do anything for each other. And you've got the damned nerve to sit there and say he was crooked."

Archer drew rein in front of the Territorial Bar. "Come in and have a drink. Cool off."

They swung down and entered the saloon. Andy was behind the bar. He placed a bottle and glasses in front of them and went back to his newspaper. Archer filled the glasses. "You know that Mike Ganoe had a shady past before he came to Silver Rock. A past that was unknown to the mine company officials. Trevor Paine dug up the dirt on Mike, throwing suspicion on Mike and you."

"So?"

"I wonder if Larry knew of Mike's past?"

"I doubt it."

"Is it possible Larry might have been suspicious of Mike – *and* you?"

"You're telling this fairy tale," Rowan said bitterly.

Archer drank his rye. "Supposing someone was watching you three that night the bullion was stolen? Waiting for you to make a break with it? Supposing greed got hold of them and they saw a chance to get away with the bullion and take care of the three men with it?"

Rowan rested his elbows on the bar. "It seems to me, Arch, that you're doing a lot of supposing?"

Arch shrugged. "Why did Ellen Farber

come back here? She was gone for years. Then suddenly she shows up, several months before you return."

"I thought you loved her, Arch."

Archer Lang studied his glass. "I did. Never figured I had much of a chance with you and Larry crowding her. I still think a lot of her. Still, there was no reason for her to come back here. Unless..." His voice trailed off.

"Unless what?"

"Unless she knows more about this thing than anyone suspects."

Rowan straightened up. "Don't push me any farther, Arch. You've been prodding me all morning. Leave Ellen out of this, you understand?"

The gambler eyed Rowan. There was no fear in him. "I've been trying to help you, Rowan."

"I'll take care of myself. Keep to your cards." Rowan turned on a heel and left the saloon. A man who had been leaning against a post at the end of the porch stood up straight and came toward Rowan. "You! Rowan Emmett!" he called. It was Durango.

Rowan turned and waited as the man came up to him. "What do you want?"

"Walt Sharpe wants to see you."

"I'm busy."

Durango's face creased into what might pass for a smile. "I said Walt Sharpe wants to see you."

Rowan took the makings from his pocket and began to fashion a cigarette. "If Walt wants to see me, he can come to me."

Durango shook his head. "You'll come with me."

Rowan smiled thinly. "Look. Walt Sharpe doesn't mean a damned thing to me. Run along and tell him so."

Durango glanced about. Men who had been lounging in front of the saloon were watching them. "You come along," he urged quietly. "I don't want to force you."

Rowan laughed. "You won't."

Durango came closer. "I know it was you who waylaid me, Emmett. I ain't forgot it."

"Don't. Or you'll get another dose. I don't like being followed, or ordered about."

Durango placed a lean, strong hand on Rowan's right forearm. Suddenly he clamped down with surprising strength and came chest to chest with Rowan. Something sharp pricked against Rowan's belly. He hadn't seen the swift movement that cleared the knife from its sheath.

"You come along quietly," said Durango, "I don't want to gut you."

A man had appeared around the corner.

56

He eased along the front of the saloon and stopped beside Durango. "All set?" he asked. His cold eyes studied Rowan.

Durango nodded. "Get behind him," he said. "No shooting, Denny."

Rowan shrugged. "All right," he said, "your argument is damned convincing." He flipped away his cigarette.

Rowan stepped back as Durango sheathed his knife. "Where is Walt?"

"Down at Cassie Whitlow's."

"Let's go."

Durango walked alongside Rowan. The man named Denny closed in behind. Rowan stepped off the end of the porch. Suddenly he whirled, smashing a right to the jaw of the squat man behind him. Denny went down hard enough to cause the dust to spurt up from the loose boards of the porch. Rowan backhanded Durango, closed in and gripped the knife wrist and then brought up a smashing uppercut that sent Durango back against the front wall of the saloon. He followed through with a blow to the gut, and, as Durango bent forward, Rowan let go of Durango's right wrist, clasped both hands together and brought them down hard on the back of Durango's neck. He raised his knee as Durango went down. The knifeman hit the knee hard and rolled sideways.

Denny leaped into action. He swung a thick arm. The blow sent Rowan reeling into the street. Before he could get his hands up, Denny hit him three times, sending him down hard. Denny grinned, revealing yellow teeth. "I'll smash you," he said, and plunged forward. Rowan got to his feet and met the rush, but Denny was a squat powerhouse. Rowan's blows seemed to have no effect. Rowan went down from a crashing blow to the jaw. Durango was on his feet now, staunching a flow of blood from the side of his mouth. He ran forward and raised a foot. The sun glinted on the cruel Mexican spur. Rowan gripped his ankle and thrust it up. Durango crashed against Denny. Rowan rolled over and got to his feet.

Durango jumped up and whipped out his knife. Denny cursed and drew his Colt. There was a crash of fire and a puff of stinking smoke. Denny grunted, dropping the Colt. Durango turned. Archer Lang stood in front of the batwings holding a smoking double-barreled derringer. "Put up the knife, Durango," he said. "Take care of your friend."

Durango spat. He sheathed the knife and gripped Denny by the arm. Blood flowed from the tips of Denny's fingers. His face was pale and he staggered a little. The smashing power of the soft-nosed slug had knocked the fight out of him. Durango whipped off his scarf and bound it about Denny's bleeding arm. He picked up the fallen Colt and walked Denny down the street. He looked back. "I'll settle you soon enough, Emmett," he said. "Orders or no orders."

Rowan wiped the blood from his face. Archer calmly reloaded his gun. "You see what I mean, Rowan?" he said quietly. "What did they want?"

Townspeople, alerted by the shot, were standing along the board sidewalks, watching Rowan. Rowan picked up his hat. "Walt Sharpe wanted to see me."

"Why in hell's name didn't you go?"

Rowan looked Archer in the eye. "I was ordered around enough at Yuma. Walt Sharpe didn't have to send two roughs after me."

Archer pocketed his gun. "It would have been easier, Rowan."

Rowan laughed shortly as he rolled a smoke. A man came swiftly toward them, carrying a sawed-off shotgun in the crook of his arm. "What the hell is going on?" he demanded. The sun glinted on the marshal's star pinned to his vest.

Archer smiled. "Nothing, Lacey," he said. "Durango and Denny Ellis had a run-in with Rowan here. Denny lost his head and drew.

You know how gun-crazy he is. I had to shoot him to stop a killing."

Lacey shook his head. "I'll have to take you in, Archer."

Rowan eyed the lean man. It was the same man he had seen in the lookout chair in the Territorial Bar. "Seems to me you showed up a little late," he said quietly. "Where were you when those two hombres jumped me?"

Lacey's gray eyes hardened. "Shut up or I'll run you in, too!"

Archer placed a hand on Rowan's shoulder. "Take it easy, Rowan," he said. "I'll go. Can't be more than a hundred dollars' fine. Wait for me."

"I'm going to see Walt."

"Not without me."

Rowan lit his cigarette. "I'll be all right. I'll pay your fine, Archer."

Archer waved a hand. "This one's on me. I always wanted to take a crack at Denny Ellis." He walked off with Lacey as though he were just going to have a drink with him.

Rowan followed them. As he neared the corner of Mesquite, he saw Ellen Farber standing in front of the newspaper office. Her face was pale. "What happened?" she asked.

Rowan took off his hat. "A little ruckus with some of Walt Sharpe's boys. Nothing serious."

She placed a hand at her throat. "Why don't you leave town, Rowan? There'll be a killing if you don't."

"It's just getting interesting, Ellen."

She shook her head. "I wish I could understand you, Rowan."

He smiled. "Why? I don't even understand myself at times."

She opened the office door. "You're a complex man, Rowan. I'd like to talk with you later. About Larry."

"Tonight?"

"Yes. I'll be here until after eight."

Rowan put on his hat and walked toward Cassie Whitlow's. He had some talking to do with Walt Sharpe before he did anything else.

CHAPTER FIVE

The bartender in Cassie's Castle told Rowan that Walt Sharpe was in Cassie's office. He leaned forward as Rowan walked toward the back of the saloon. "He's already heard about the ruckus you had with Durango and Denny Ellis. Thought you'd like to know."

Rowan waved a hand. "Thanks, *amigo*. Is he alone?"

61

"Him and Cassie."

"No gunmen?"

The barkeep shook his head. "I'm expecting Durango and Ellis, though."

Rowan grinned crookedly. "It'll be a while before Ellis gets here. He's wearing a .41 caliber slug in his arm, courtesy of Archer Lang."

The barkeep paled. "I hope there won't be no shooting here, Emmett."

Rowan shook his head. "Not as long as Walt thinks I've got something he wants. Best insurance in Silver Rock." Rowan entered the hall and tapped on Cassie's door. "Come in," she called.

Walt Sharpe was seated near the one window, dragging on a big cigar. Cassie was at her desk, her face pale. The tobacco smoke hung in rifted layers in the small room. Sharpe pointed to a chair. "Set," he said quietly.

Rowan sat down and lit a cigarette. "What do you want, Sharpe?" he asked.

Sharpe's heavy lids raised. "I sent the boys after you. What happened?"

"They got rough. Arch Lang took a hand."

"I didn't want any trouble."

Rowan leaned forward. "The next time you want to see me, just send a message or come and see me yourself. I don't like the roughs you feed, Walt."

Sharpe inspected his cigar. "I usually don't have to plead with a man to come and see *me*, Rowan."

Cassie looked away. There was a look of disgust on her painted face. "Rowan Emmett isn't afraid of you, Walt. Do you think every man in Silver Rock is afraid of you?"

Sharpe turned slowly. "Shut up!" he said.

"What do you want, Walt?" asked Rowan. There was an impulse creeping up on him to sink his fists into Walt's fat belly and knock some of the wind and conceit out of him.

Sharpe crossed a fat leg and carefully adjusted the crease in his fine trousers. "I offered you a proposition, Emmett. I've waited patiently for an answer."

"You already got an answer."

The dark eyes held Rowan's. "Not the one I want."

"It's the only one you'll get."

Sharpe relit his cigar. "Let's put the cards on the table, shall we?" he suggested. "You're safe in town as long as you keep the information to yourself. However, my patience can wear thin."

"So? Supposing I leave Silver Rock?"

The dark eyes were partly covered when Sharpe spoke again. "How far do you think you'd get?"

"I can take care of myself."

Walt nodded. "To a certain extent. You'll let your guard down some day. Arch Lang won't always be around to help you, either."

"I'll take my chances."

"Talk to him, Cassie," said Sharpe.

Cassie leaned forward. "He means it, Rowan. Why don't you work with him?"

Rowan eyed the woman. "What's in it for you, Cassie?"

She flushed. "We could go away together. Or you could throw in with me. I need a good man around here. I've got ideas. I'll move up on Bonanza again and have a real tony joint. We can make money, Rowan." There was a desperate tone in her voice.

Rowan laughed. "The boom days are gone, Cassie. They'll never come back."

"Walt says he plans to invest in some steam pumps. Big ones. He says he can clear the mines again."

"He's loco."

Sharpe shook his head. "I can get some pumps with a capacity of millions of gallons a day. The mines will open again. You and Cassie could clean up."

"You've been chewing peyote buttons, Walt."

"Damn you! I've fooled around enough! You either come through in twenty-four hours or you'll end up on Boot Hill!" Sharpe stood up and threw his cigar on the floor. He ground it with a heel. "That's my last warning."

Rowan grinned. "Stop acting like a he-man, Walt. You haven't got the guts or the shape for it."

Sharpe walked to the door. "I've said my piece, Emmett. The rest is up to you." He slammed the door behind him.

Cassie lit a cigarette and filled two glasses from a decanter. She handed Rowan a glass. "Why must you antagonize him, Rowan? He's dangerous."

Rowan studied her. "Why are you siding with him?"

She downed her drink and took another. "I'll tell you the truth, Rowan. I had plenty of money when I left here. Lost all of it gambling. Walt set me up in this place. He asked me to speak with you."

"You can walk out on him."

Her face seemed to relax, showing all of her years, so bravely covered by carefully applied make-up. Rowan suddenly realized that all of Cassie Whitlow's bravado was gone, leaving her a shell of a woman, a badly frightened woman. "I can't," she said. "I've always lived well. The best of everything. Liquor, clothes, furnishings and plenty of money to throw away. It's all gone now. I'm getting old. If I lose this place you know where I'll end up."

"You can always find a good man, Cassie."

For a moment hope flashed across her face and then she looked away. "You? Archer Lang? I know better. No one would take me now, Rowan. I've got to stand on my own feet. Supposing the mines *do* open once more. I'd be on top of the pile again."

Rowan glanced at the whisky decanter. "You keep on with that stuff and you know what pile you'll end up on, Cassie."

She filled her glass again, looking defiantly at him. "I can hold it," she said.

"Now, perhaps. Suddenly it will hold you."

"Oh, be quiet!"

Rowan shrugged and picked up his hat. She turned quickly. "Wait! Rowan, listen to me! I'll help you."

"How?"

Her face worked a little. "Look, you know where the silver is. I've got friends who come in here. Men who'll do anything I ask them to. You get the silver and I'll have good men to help you get it out of town. Walt isn't king here in Silver Rock. What do you say?"

He stood up and looked down at her as she emptied and refilled her glass. "I told you I don't know where it is."

"You're lying to me!"

A feeling of disgust came over him. "The bottle is talking," he said.

She got to her feet and rounded the desk, lashing out with her right hand. It smacked against Rowan's face. He gripped her wrist and forced her arm down. "Sober up," he said.

For a moment she struggled against him and then came close, raising her face. "Kiss me," she said huskily. Her breath was sour with liquor fumes. Rowan released her wrist. "Get some coffee," he said and turned to the door. She gripped his coat. "I know what you're up to," she said thickly. "You and that stuck-up Farber woman. Her with her martyred air. Well, you won't get out of Silver Rock with that bullion! I'll see to that!"

"So long, Cassie." Rowan closed the door and shook his head as he heard her curse. There was a smash of glass, and the door shook a little. "Wasting good liquor, Cassie!" he called, and went into the saloon. Durango was standing at the bar. He turned his swollen face toward Rowan. Rowan slipped his right hand underneath his coat. "Well?" he asked, softly. Durango looked away. Rowan smiled and left the saloon, sauntering slowly toward Bonanza. Things were shaping up, and as yet he had no inkling as to where the bullion was. He looked up to see Hardtack Christie seated at the edge of a porch.

Christie beckoned to Rowan. "Want a talk with you," he said.

"You, too?"

Hardtack scratched in his beard. "What's eatin' you?"

Rowan waved a hand airily. "The whole damned town."

Hardtack waved Rowan to follow him and set off down an alley. "Come on down to my place." He led the way to a sagging jacale and went in. Rowan followed and grinned as he looked about. Hardtack's famous checkered vest, fork-tailed coat and battered silk hat hung on wooden pegs. The ebony cane, minus the famous gold knob, leaned in a corner. Dust rose from the blankets as Rowan sat down on a sagging cot. Hardtack opened a bottle and filled two tin cups. "I was thinkin' a lot about you, Rowan."

"So?"

"My memory ain't what it used to be. Fergit a lot of things."

"Except Angie."

Hardtack raised his bushy eyebrows. "Now how did you know *that?*"

Rowan smiled. "How could anyone forget Angie?"

Hardtack lowered his brows. "You mean *you* know *her* too?"

68

"No, thank heaven."

Hardtack grunted. "Yeah. Yeah. Howsomever, I been doin' some thinkin'. You remember me being in town when the robbery of the silver was done?"

"You were on a three-day toot, I think."

"Five," said Hardtack solemnly. "*Never* less than five. I ain't no tinhorn!"

"Keep talking."

Hardtack cut a chew and stuffed it into his mouth, working it into pliability. "Seems to me I saw something that night of the robbery." He shifted his chew. "I was broke again, as usual, and couldn't get any *dinero* in a hurry, although I had plenty cached out in the desert. Never trusted no banks."

"Just Angie."

"Yeah. Yeah. Just Angie. Anyways, I was broke. I'll finish this yet, if you keep your mouth shut. I needed *dinero*. I walked outta town and headed up the arroyo east of here, for the slope there below the hills. Had a few diggin' tools with me. Figured one of them damned drifts from the mine must be so close to the surface there a man could cut through and get some ore."

Rowan raised his brows. "Hardtack! You? A high-grader?"

"Yeah. Yeah. A damned *gambosino*." He

69

looked defiantly at Rowan. "It was my mine, wasn't it? Got a measly hundred thousand for it. Swindled, I was."

"Sure were, *amigo*."

"Well, I was figuring out the set of the drift when I thought I'd better have a drink or two to help me. Damned if I didn't pass out. Coupla hours later I was awakened by the sound of hoofbeats. I was worried, figuring them damned scoundrels that stole my mine might have a patrol or something out, watching for high-graders. I hid in the brush. There was a faint moon that night, as you might recall."

Rowan nodded. He needed no spur to his memory about *that* night.

"Pretty soon I saw two *hombres* ride past," continued Hardtack, " 'bout fifty yards away. I lay low. Half an hour later I decided I'd better get outta there. Hid my tools and took my jug. The moon was full up by then. I followed the wash and saw the hoof prints. The sand was still damp from the rain of the day before. Checked the hoof prints. Old habit of mine. Figured there were five horses – or mules – that had gone through there. Weren't no hoof marks when I came *up* the arroyo and into the wash."

Rowan leaned forward. "You're sure?"

"Positive. Anyways, I kept away from the

road. Mighta found you if I *had* gone to the road. Being nosy, I backtracked down the wash to the edge of the hills, following the tracks. Moon was behind clouds then. About two hundred yards from where I had been hiding I could hear sounds of digging. Damned high-graders, I figured. I was going to take a closer look when I remembered I had left my gun where I hid the tools. Didn't want no trouble, so I looked for the gun and couldn't find it. Headed back for town. Got drunk. Went on another five-day toot – on credit – and then headed out into the desert after another strike. Never found it. Came back to Silver Rock a coupla months later and heard about you."

Rowan refilled his cup. "What's the connection?"

Hardtack rubbed his jaw. "You figure them *hombres* on the hosses might have had something to do with you?"

"It's possible."

"Looky here," said Hardtack. He leaned forward and tapped Rowan's knee with a finger. "First I saw two men riding. Then I find tracks of five horses, or mules. Three of them horses or mules were loaded heavy. You follow now?"

Sweat worked down Rowan's sides. "Yes. You didn't see the loaded horses, did you?"

71

"As I said – I saw two men riding. Found tracks of five animals."

Rowan sipped his liquor. "Can you show me where they were digging?"

Hardtack shrugged. "Trouble is I can't exactly remember."

"You left your tools there."

"Yeah. Yeah. Never went back for 'em either."

"Maybe they're still lying there."

"I doubt it. Somebody might have picked them up. Mebbe the sand drifted over 'em. That was ten years ago. Mind?"

Rowan stood up. "It's worth a look. Will you come with me?"

Hardtack drained his cup. "You ain't goin' out there now, are you?"

"No. How about tonight?"

"Keno."

"You working?"

"Not until tomorrow morning."

Rowan stood up. "Keep your mouth shut, Hardtack. If this is a lead and we find the silver I'll make it worth your while."

"You keeping it for yourself?" asked Hardtack slyly.

"Hell no! That silver will clear me."

"It won't clear you of Larry Farber's killin'."

"*Quien sabe?*"

72

"Yeah. Yeah."

Rowan gripped the old man by the shoulder. "Keep away from the jug today and tonight, Hardtack. If you help me find that bullion I'll see to it that you get all the redeye you want."

Hardtack raised a dirty hand. "I swear I will," he said.

Rowan left the filthy shack. He looked up and down the alley. There was no one in sight. As he walked toward the street he saw a partially consumed cigarette butt still smoking on the hard earth. A cold feeling came over him. He walked up Mesquite to Bonanza. The town was sleeping in the sun. Rowan went to the hotel. Archer Lang was asleep on his bed. Rowan sat down near a front window and went over what Hardtack had said. It might mean nothing – still, it was all he had to go on.

Archer opened his eyes. "Where the hell have you been?"

"Talked with Walt Sharpe. Walt thinks he can scare me into telling him where the silver is."

"How can he if you don't know?"

"He's got a one-track mind, Arch. Did you pay your fine?"

"One hundred."

Rowan peeled five twenties from the roll

73

Cassie had given him and placed it on the table. Archer grinned. He sat up and took three of the twenties, taking a ten from his wallet. He placed the ten with the two other twenties and shoved them toward Rowan. "I'll split," he said, "I enjoyed plugging Ellis. It would have pleasured me more to let some blood out of Durango, but you can't have everything."

Rowan leaned back in the chair. He saw Durango enter the Territorial Bar. "Did you know Walt Sharpe staked Cassie Whitlow so she could open her place?"

Archer yawned. "I suspected it."

"Does Sharpe actually intend to pump out the mines?"

Archer sat up. "Yes. But I think he's broke. Or close to it. He's getting desperate, Rowan. I'm into him for five thousand dollars in gambling debts. Cassie's place isn't paying off too well. Sharpe owes Amos Darby quite a sum. You can see why he wants that fifty thousand now."

Rowan nodded. "He said I'd never get away from Silver Rock if I tried."

"Do you intend to?"

"You know me better than that."

"Have you any leads on the silver?"

Rowan looked out of the window. "No," he lied.

"I see. What do you intend to do?"

Rowan shrugged. "Wait for a lead."

"It might be a long wait. Sharpe will be pushing you. Amos Darby is itching for some of that bullion."

"Let him itch."

"I'd like to see you get it as quickly as possible."

Rowan turned slowly. "You've been a good friend, Archer."

Archer lit a cigarette. "Forget it. I haven't got a real friend in Silver Rock. Outside of Ellen Farber, that is." He looked at Rowan.

"You're still in love with her?"

"Yes."

"I'm seeing her tonight, Archer."

"I expected you to see her."

Rowan shoved back his hat. "I have no plans for Ellen and myself, Archer."

The gambler held out his slim hands, palms upward. "Even if you did, there is nothing I can say about it. She still loves you, Rowan. I'm sure of that, at least."

"You may be wrong."

"I wish I was. How about dinner with me this evening?"

"Yes."

"There'll be a good game at the Territorial tonight."

"I might drop in after I see Ellen."

75

"*Bueno*. Now I'm due for some sleep. I've had a run of good luck and I mean to keep it going. It may be a long game tonight ... for high stakes." Archer lay down and closed his eyes.

Rowan nodded. He had a game tonight, for higher stakes than in Archer's game. He hoped to God Hardtack had uncovered something for him to work on.

CHAPTER SIX

It was a little before eight when Rowan stopped outside of the newspaper office. He could see Ellen Farber at her desk. Beyond her was Jim Bond, writing busily. Rowan glanced up and down the street. Everything was quiet. He touched the Colt thrust beneath his waistband, then opened the door. Ellen smiled as she looked up. Jim Bond nodded and shoved back his work. "I was writing an account of today's shooting," he said. "Would you like to hear the rough draft?"

Rowan nodded. He sat down where he could watch Ellen's profile. She clasped her slender hands together and rested her chin on them. It was a typical position of hers, Rowan

76

remembered. Ellen had a way of listening to a man as though everything he said was of the utmost importance. Hanging on the wall beside her desk was a photograph of Larry. There was a faint smile on his handsome face. It was almost as though he were welcoming Rowan.

Jim cleared his throat. "Does law and order exist in Silver Rock," he read quickly, "or have we reverted to the old boom days? Today two roughs, employed by one of the town's leading citizens, Mr. Walter Sharpe, attempted to strong-arm Mr. Rowan Emmett, who is visiting here. In the ensuing struggle, Mr. Emmett, while giving a good account of himself, was downed. Had not Mr. Archer Lang come to his rescue, there might have been a killing on the streets of Silver Rock. The two roughs, one known only as Durango, the other Denny Ellis, had the worst of the encounter. Mr. Ellis is recovering from a bullet wound in the right forearm. The editor of this paper does not condone Mr. Lang's impetuous action in shooting before attempting other means of helping Mr. Emmett, but it might have saved the life of Mr. Emmett." Jim glanced up at Rowan.

"Amen," said Rowan quietly.

"City Marshal Dan Lacey arrived in time to prevent more bloodshed. Mr. Lang was fined

77

one hundred dollars for discharging a firearm within the city limits. Durango and Ellis were not incarcerated. Is it possible that our laws allow such episodes to occur on the streets of Silver Rock? Two hard-case characters waylay and beat a man and are not punished in any respect. Mr. Lang, who courageously came to the help of his friend, was forced to pay a heavy fine. The editor of this paper has it on good authority that City Marshal Dan Lacey saw the strong-arm attempt on Mr. Emmett and bided his time until the shooting occurred. It has long been the opinion of this paper that Marshal Dan Lacey, who is also employed by Mr. Amos Darby of the Territorial Bar as a lookout man for his thriving games of chance, should either resign from his position of City Marshal or cease his employment by Mr. Darby. City Marshal Lacey seems only to act as a police officer when such actions do not interfere in the interests of Mr. Sharpe and Mr. Darby. Our city has come a long way from the days when courageous, honest marshals such as Halford Pierce, Andrew Becket, Samuel Afton and Rowan Emmett wore the star, played no favorites and backed the city ordinances to the letter." Jim looked up at Rowan. "Well?"

Rowan rubbed his jaw. "You're preaching fire and brimstone, Jim. Aren't you a little afraid some of it might run off on you?"

Jim shook his head. "This paper will crusade for what is right, Rowan."

"I see your point. But you're not a fighting man – by that, a *gun* man. In that editorial you've antagonized Walt Sharpe Amos Darby, Dan Lacey, Durango and Denny Ellis. You're looking for trouble."

"I told him that," said Ellen quietly.

Jim took up his pencil. "With a little revision and a few more choice statements this editorial will appear in tomorrow's newspaper."

Rowan leaned back in his chair and fashioned a cigarette. "How many people in Silver Rock think as you do?"

Jim waved a hand. "Most of them."

"How many of them will back you up if some of those you mention in the editorial decide to take action against you?"

"I think most of them will."

Rowan shook his head. "I doubt it. From the looks of things here in town I can see where a few men are ruling the roost. Unless you have an organized body to stand against them you'll suffer for it one way or another. A beating, a wrecking of your press, or perhaps worse. Why don't you hold off awhile, Jim?"

"This is hot news, Rowan. I've been waiting for a chance to get at those men."

Rowan shook his head. "Get some of the honest men in town aside. Talk with them. Form a Vigilante Committee if you have to. Let your opposition know you are not alone. They'll think twice before they attack you."

"Would you work with us, Rowan?"

"No."

Ellen glanced quickly at Rowan. "Why not?"

"You know my position. A jailbird. You can't even consider me as a citizen of Silver Rock. Besides, I came here for a far different purpose."

Jim lit a cigar. "What have you found out since your return?"

"Nothing of importance."

Jim puffed at his cigar. "But you've felt the way Sharpe and others feel about you. Perhaps, by working on your Vigilante Committee, you might be able to clear yourself more rapidly."

Ellen's gray eyes held Rowan's. It was plain that she wanted Rowan to agree with Jim Bond. Rowan ground out his cigarette. "I'll work alone," he said, "and wait until I do clear myself. Then, and *only* then, will I help you."

Jim shrugged. "Perhaps you're right."

"You'll hold off on that editorial then?"

Jim smiled. "You misunderstood me. I'll

agree that perhaps this isn't the right time for you to fight against the interests that control Silver Rock, but it is for me. The editorial will appear in the paper tomorrow afternoon."

"You're looking for serious trouble, Jim."

"I've been in trouble before, Rowan."

"The pen is mightier than the sword. Is that it?"

"I follow that theory."

"The pen might not be mightier than a forty-four slug in the back, Jim."

Jim stood up. "I'm going ahead," he said quietly. "Will you see Ellen home? I'll be working late tonight."

Rowan helped Ellen with her coat. They stepped out into the street. Two men stood in front of Cassie Whitlow's, arguing in loud, drunken voices. Ellen glanced at them. "Our esteemed city marshal is now on duty at the Territorial Bar," she said bitterly. "Anything can happen on the streets of Silver Rock at night."

Rowan took her by the arm, experiencing a thrill despite himself. "Jim is a brave man, but a fool," he said. "Why can't he wait?"

"Some men can't wait. Perhaps we owe much to that sort of man. There are not enough of them."

"Perhaps you think I should have worked with him?"

"It would have taken courage."

"Meaning I lack courage?"

She shook her head. "Not the type we are accustomed to out here in the Southwest. You're a man skilled in gun play and with your fists. As good as any man in Silver Rock. Jim can't handle a gun. He doesn't even own one. That seems incredible to you, doesn't it?"

"Yes."

She glanced back at the lamplit office. "His courage is deeper, deserving more respect than your kind, but few people realize that. It is for history to show their true worth."

Rowan nodded. She was right, but there was no changing his mind. Ten years in Yuma had set his feet on the trail he must follow to the dark end, or into the light. Ellen bent her head toward a boardinghouse set back from the street. "This is where I live," she said. "Let's sit on the porch for a while. I want to talk with you." She led the way.

Rowan sat down in a comfortable chair. Below them the street dipped down toward the center of town. The yellow lamplight etched rectangles against the darkness. A cool wind felt its way along the street, raising whorls of dust in the corners. Ellen rested her head against the back of her chair and closed her eyes.

"Do you like Silver Rock?" she asked.

"I used to."

"Because of the night life here? Because of your friends? Or did the town itself appeal to you?"

Rowan shrugged. "I never thought of that. It was a boom town. I had a good job. My luck was good at the gaming tables."

"If you had not gone to prison it's likely that you wouldn't have stayed here after the mines flooded."

"Probably not."

She shifted, turning her head to look at him. "In time Silver Rock will come to life again, not as a boom town, but as a trading center for the many ranches and new farms in this area."

Rowan looked quickly at her. "Yes?"

She rested her hand on his wrist. "I'd like to stay here," she said, "but not as it is today. That is why I wanted you to work with Jim."

"You know my reason for not doing so."

"I had hoped differently."

Rowan rested his arms on the porch rail and looked toward the dim outline of the hills beyond the town. "You said you wanted to talk about Larry, Ellen. Seems to me we're doing a lot of talking about *me*. What is it you wanted to tell me?"

She leaned toward him. "A story circulated

around town during your trial that you had killed Larry because I married him instead of you. Did you know that?"

"Yes. I never gave it a second thought."

"It might have swayed the jury."

"That's possible."

"I'm sure it did."

He shrugged. "It doesn't make any difference now."

"You and Larry were such good friends. Damon and Pythias."

He grinned. "I've got you there, Ellen. Read about those two *hombres* while in prison. Did a lot of reading there. Improving my mind."

"Yet you never really did know Larry. Not the inside of Larry."

Something in her tone caused him to turn. "What do you mean?"

She hesitated. "A wife knows a man quite differently from the way his friends – or even his mother – do."

"Go on."

She bowed her head. "I've never spoken of this to anyone before. Do you know why Larry *really* married me?"

"That's a silly question, isn't it, Ellen?"

"No," she said in a low voice. "Larry married me because he was always a little jealous of you. *You* never knew it. You valued his friendship much more than he did yours."

He stood up. "I've heard enough," he said.

She grasped his sleeve, and the touch was repulsive to him. "Listen," she said. "Do you think it's easy for me to tell you this? The shame of it has hung like a cloud in my mind. Larry didn't really want me, Rowan. Do you understand? I knew it on our wedding night. If you had heard what he said!"

"Stop, Ellen!"

She stood up. "No. What I have to tell you may help you, Rowan. You stood aside when Larry showed his interest in me. You were always too generous. Everything for your friends, that was Rowan Emmett. You were a fool then, Rowan. I had hoped you'd changed by now."

"I've changed, all right."

She came close. "What I'm trying to tell you, and making a terrible botch of it, is this — Larry was never really your friend. After he had me, he saw that he hadn't really hurt you enough."

He gripped the porch rail hard. "Get done with it," he said, "so I can leave."

"I'm trying to give you a lead, Rowan. What I'm telling you cuts me like a knife, but I *must* tell you."

"You've done fine so far," he said bitterly.

She stepped back. "I don't know the truth

about the theft of the bullion nor the death of Mike Ganoe. All I do know is this – you were never capable of those crimes."

"Thanks for *that*, anyway." Rowan picked up his hat and walked to the stairs.

She came up behind him. "You don't believe me, Rowan?"

"You make me sick!"

She swallowed hard. "I came back to Silver Rock to help you. Don't you realize that?"

"I find it hard to believe. Defiling the name of the man who was closer to me than my own brothers."

"You were a fool. Larry Farber never thought of anyone but himself. He was selfish, cruel and insanely jealous of you!"

Rowan's right hand came up before he realized it. For one terrible moment his hand was poised to slap the pretty face in front of him. With a strong will he lowered his hand. Cold sweat broke out on his face.

"Hitting me won't change the truth," she said wearily. "I failed." She turned away. "Good night, Rowan."

He did not answer as he went down the stairs. She was still standing there when he reached the corner of the alleyway that led to Hardtack's jacale.

The jacale was dark when Rowan saw it. He tapped on the door. It swung open easily with a faint creak of leather hinges. "Hardtack!" called Rowan. The place stank of sour whisky slops, greasy food and unwashed clothing. Rowan lit a match and cupped it in his hands. The place was empty. He closed the door behind him and started swiftly for the street. The damned idiot surely wasn't standing at a bar guzzling again. Not tonight!

Rowan looked in at the Barrel House, the Yucca and the Silver Nugget. Hardtack wasn't in any of them. He crossed the street to the Territorial Bar and looked in through a flyspecked window. The place was busy, but Hardtack wasn't in sight. There was one other place he could be. Cassie Whitlow's. Rowan strode down Bonanza. He turned the corner and stepped over a drunk who was sprawled across the walk. He looked over the batwings of Cassie's place. Hardtack was leaning against the end of the bar, staring moodily at an empty glass. Four men were playing poker at a rear table. One of the girls was asleep in a chair. Another was seated on the lap of a bearded man, whispering into his ear. Two cowpokes stood at the bar.

Rowan pushed through the batwings. He stopped beside Hardtack. "You damned idiot," he said, "I thought you'd have enough sense to stay sober."

"I got to thinking of Angie."

87

"I'll meet you at the livery stable."

"Not until I get a double rye."

For a moment Rowan felt like slugging the old reprobate. He called to the bartender. "Rye," he said. "A double for the old-timer here."

The bartender filled the glasses. "Better get out of here, Rowan," he said. "Denny Ellis is in a back room, talking war. He hasn't got the brains of a damned jackass but he's full of enough redeye to start shooting if he sees you or Archer Lang."

"Thanks. I'll leave." Rowan trod heavily on Hardtack's toes and left the saloon. He walked slowly back to the livery stable. The night man looked up from a game of solitaire. "You want your cayuse?" he asked.

Rowan placed a twenty on the table. "Yes. Saddle a horse for Hardtack Christie, too."

The man scratched his chin. "Hardtack? That bum a friend of yours?"

"In a way."

"That so?"

Rowan placed his hands flat on the table. "I'm riding out of here right now. You get that horse for Hardtack. Keep your mouth shut and the twenty is yours. If you talk I'll take it back and take twenty dollars' worth out of your hide. Understand?"

The liveryman shoved the twenty toward

Rowan. "You don't remember me, Emmett, but onct, years ago, you kept me from getting my head beat in in a brawl at the Yucca. Your money ain't no good with me." He stood up and walked into the stable, saddled Smoky and stepped back. "I'll get the sorrel for Hardtack. Hope you find what you're looking for, Emmett."

Rowan led the roan out the back door. Trying to work his problem out secretly in Silver Rock was almost impossible. He led the roan down to Yucca and then toward the east side of town. He waited at the edge of town. In a few minutes he heard the beat of hoofs on the baked earth, and a horseman appeared. It was Hardtack. He raised a hand in salute. "First time I been on a cayuse in over a year," he said.

"See that you stay on it," said Rowan. "Anyone see you?"

"Not that I know of."

"Keno. Let's get going." Rowan mounted and led the way out of the Creek Road. The wind was cold, searching through his clothing. Hardtack shivered. "Shoulda brought a bottle," he said sourly. "Damned poor time of the night to be looking for things."

"There'll be a moon later. Stop griping."

They reached the arroyo and Hardtack took

the lead. Half a mile from the road he drew rein. "Somewhere around here it was," he said.

Rowan swung down. "Get down. We'll have a smoke until the moon comes up."

Hardtack dismounted, eyed Rowan and then felt inside his ragged coat. He brought out a pint bottle. "Cough medicine," he said apologetically. "My tubes get clogged in the night air."

"You sure it isn't your head gets clogged up, Hardtack?"

The old man waggled his head and pried out the cork. "Never at night. Only in the morning after a few drinks. Have a snort?"

Rowan took the bottle and drank. He passed it back to Hardtack. The old man drank deeply, replaced the cork, felt about on the ground until he found a clear spot and eased himself down. "Wake me when the moon gets up," he said.

Rowan rolled a smoke. Ellen's words came back to him. He rebuilt a picture of Larry Ferber in his mind. Always laughing, always solicitous of Rowan. How *could* she be right? Yet there had been the ring of truth in her words. The answer would never be found. Larry Farber was long dead now. Rowan lit his cigarette and leaned back against a rock. A wife knows a man quite differently from the way his friends – or even his mother – do, she had said. Larry didn't really want me, Rowan. No woman, particularly Ellen, would have admitted that to any man. Rowan shook his head. Her words kept coming back to him – he was selfish, cruel and insanely jealous of you. Rowan turned quickly. It was almost as though she stood behind him in the darkness, breathing the words into his ear. He reached for the bottle, drank deeply and closed his eyes. "Damn her!" he said savagely.

CHAPTER SEVEN

The moon rose slowly from behind the mountains to the east, silvering the desert, bringing shadows into sharp relief. Rowan shook Hardtack. "Rise and shine, Hardtack," he said. "Shake a leg! Hit the dirt!"

Hardtack groaned. "Angie," he said mournfully. He opened his eyes. He reached for the bottle and took a slug. "Helluva note, Rowan. An old man like me drug out here on the desert at night. You'll clog my tubes for sure."

"Shut up. Give me that bottle." Rowan placed it in his coat pocket. "Let's get going!"

The old man limped down the wash, eying the eroded banks. "Wasn't too far from here." He looked up at the low hills that were close to the wash. In places the wash had cut deep into the hills, forming vertical walls. Hardtack moved back and forth, mumbling to himself, stepping back to eye the hills and then looking close along the west bank of the wash. "Damned place has changed in ten years," he said. "Rowan, I ain't sure about this at all."

Rowan had a sinking feeling as he eyed the bank. The flash storms of ten years would have altered the place to such an extent that even Hardtack could never find the place where he had left his tools and gun.

Hardtack scrambled up the east bank and studied the hills. Rowan climbed up beside him. In the silvery light of the moon they could see the distant mine structures and the long line of hills that trended from west to east like the serrated back of some great antediluvian monster, three quarters buried in the earth. They were ugly, treeless hills, a drab monotony of large rocks and boulders, stippled with sparse mesquite and cactus growth. It was hard to believe in the great fortunes of silver which had been ripped from their bowels.

Hardtack cut a chew and squatted on a

rock. He looked like a wise old owl as he eyed the hills. "Yuh see," he said. "Look along them hills. Helluva long time ago, thousands of years mebbe, them hills sank down at this end."

"About the time you were in diapers, Hardtack?"

"Go to hell!"

"Keep talking, Dad."

Hardtack shifted his chew. "Anyways, the silver was in there when it happened. So, yuh see, the mine drifts start high up, 'bout where the center of the hills is. *So,* to dig the ore, some of them drifts came down this way at a slant. Now, from what I remember, some of them drifts must end damned close to where we are now. Almost at the surface in some places. I mind one time when a drift collapsed, burying two Cousin Jacks. Had a helluva time trying to get them out until Dusty Innes left the mine, walked over the hills, and showed the boys a sunken spot. They dug down and found the buried men. So yuh see how close to the surface some of them is."

Rowan nodded. He remembered falling into the great open stope on Fourth Street. "That was why you figured you'd cut in somewhere for your high-grading."

"Yeah. Thought I'd have me a nice little

93

hidden entrance here where I could get some of my own ore back." Hardtack slid down the slope and began to cast back and forth like a sad-looking hunting hound. "Dammit! It's close hereabouts, but I ain't sure."

Rowan rolled a smoke while watching the old man. Half an hour drifted past. Suddenly Rowan raised his head. He turned. Some subtle warning had come to him through the night. The flats to the east were empty, clearly lit by the moon. Each bush stood out sharply, its shadow etched in the ground. Rowan walked to the east and stopped to listen. Somewhere to his left he thought his eye caught a quick, furtive movement. He watched the spot, but nothing happened. A coyote, maybe, prowling for food. He walked back to the wash and then suddenly turned. Again he saw the movement. He slid down into the wash. "Any luck, Hardtack?" he asked.

Hardtack scratched in his beard. "I'll find it yet."

"Forget it for tonight."

"You loco? I'll find it! Trouble with you is you got no patience."

Rowan came close to the old man. "Someone is out in the brush," he said softly.

Hardtack nodded. "Okay. Let's go. Too

damned cold out here for an old man like me."

Rowan got the horses. They rode back toward the road. There was the sound of a breaking stick. The echo of a shot boomed back from the hills. Rowan crouched low. Hardtack cursed. "You hit?" called Rowan.

"Hell no! But that slug fanned my face!"

Rowan saw a puff of smoke drifting through the brush. It was too far for a pistol shot. He eyed the smoke. Something moved in the brush. Then he heard the thud of hoofs. A thread of dust wavered up.

"Damned drygulcher," said Hardtack.

Rowan rubbed his jaw. He felt as though every movement he made was under surveillance. "Who did he shoot at?" he mused aloud.

"Why ... *you* ... dammit!" Hardtack looked quickly at Rowan as they reached the Creek Road.

Rowan placed a hand on the cantle of his saddle and looked back along the road. "Yes. I guess so."

"What the hell you drivin' at? You think they was after *me*?"

"You know too damned much about the mines around here, Hardtack."

"Yeah. That's why that shot wasn't aimed at me. Wouldn't do anyone any good to kill *me*. It was for you, sonny, and don't you try to worry me by making out they tried to get me."

Rowan grinned. "Maybe it was Angie," he said.

Hardtack slapped his thigh. "You got something there! She was right handy with a gun, as I remember."

They rode into town, left their horses at the stable and then separated. Rowan was no closer to the lost bullion than on the first day he had come to Silver Rock.

Rowan got up early, while Archer Lang was still asleep. He left the hotel and ate breakfast. The waitress left a copy of the newspaper on the table. Rowan eyed the headline. "There is no law in Silver Rock," he read aloud. He scanned the editorial. It was just as Jim had read it to him. He finished his breakfast and went out into the street, stopping to fashion a smoke. He saw Dan Lacey step out of the Territorial Bar and walk swiftly toward the newspaper office. A folded newspaper was under his arm. Rowan threw down his unfinished cigarette and followed the lawman.

Dan Lacey walked down the center of the street, his boot heels rapping sharply. He looked to neither side. Rowan was thirty feet behind him when he stepped up on the board sidewalk in front of the office and opened the door. It banged against the wall and stayed open. Rowan stopped outside. Jim Bond looked up as he saw Lacey. "Hello, Dan," he said. Ellen Farber placed a slim hand at her throat and eyed the angry marshal.

Lacey threw the paper down on the counter. "I've warned you about this sort of thing before, Bond," he said.

Bond raised his eyebrows. "So you have."

"You'll take back every paper you find and then publish an apology in your next edition!"

Bond stood up and placed his hands flat on the counter. "Do you deny the fact that you stayed out of the way while Rowan Emmett was being bullied by Durango and Ellis? Do you deny the fact that you work for Amos Darby as a lookout when you should be on duty in the streets?"

Lacey reached his left hand across the counter and gripped Bond by the front of his coat. He reached down for his Colt. Rowan stepped into the office. "All right, Lacey," he said, "calm down."

Lacey released Bond and turned quickly. "Maybe you want a piece of this pistol-whipping too?"

Rowan leaned against the door and took the makings from his shirt pocket. "No, and what's more there won't be *any* pistol-whipping done at all."

Lacey's face tightened into a set smile. "You like to throw your weight around, jailbird."

Rowan lit his smoke and eyed Lacey over the flare of the match. "Put that cutter down on the counter and step out into the street, and we'll see *whose* weight gets thrown around, tinhorn."

Lacey closed his fists. "I'm on duty," he said.

Rowan threw back his head and laughed. "This town was always good for a laugh in the old days. It hasn't changed. Even the marshals are comics."

Lacey dropped his hand to his Colt. "Get out of my way," he said.

Rowan looked down at Lacey's gun hand. "You wouldn't draw on me, would you, Lacey? Not while I'm facing you without a gun?"

"There's an ordinance in this town against firearms being carried by those without permits."

Rowan grinned. "There sure are a lot of permits, compared to the old days."

Lacey raised his head. "I can run you in for carrying a concealed cutter. Maybe I will."

Rowan yawned. He reached slowly into his

coat pocket, watching Lacey's eyes. Rowan withdrew his wallet and removed a card from it. "Here's my permit," he said, "Dated over ten years ago."

"It ain't legal now."

"So? It never was revoked, according to my knowledge."

Lacey flushed and walked toward Rowan. Rowan stepped aside. Lacey turned at the door. "Bond, we'll settle this soon enough."

Jim Bond shrugged.

Lacey looked Rowan full in the eye. "Your day is coming too, *hombre*." He left the office.

Bond loosened his collar and wiped the sweat from his face. "He sure was riled, Rowan."

Rowan nodded. "I advised you to lay off that editorial for a while. You expected someone to come in here primed for a brawl, didn't you?"

Bond nodded. "I suppose I should have been more careful in what I wrote. Still . . ." Bond slammed a clenched fist down on the counter. "I'm a newspaperman! As long as there is freedom of the press I'll print the naked truth!"

Rowan shrugged. "You'd better organize a citizen's committee, or a group of vigilantes. You'll need help." He looked at Ellen. She flushed and looked down at her work. Rowan left the office.

He walked around the corner of Bonanza and Mesquite and looked into Hardtack's shack. The place was empty. Then he remembered that the old man was probably at work, swamping at the Territorial. He headed for the saloon.

The Territorial was empty except for Andy, the barkeep, who was leaning against the end of the bar. Hardtack's mop and bucket were near the front door. Rowan slapped his hand on the bar. "Where's Hardtack, Andy?" he asked.

Andy's faded eyes flicked away from Rowan's direct gaze. "He ain't here, Rowan."

Rowan glanced at the bucket and mop. "Who's swamping today?"

"Huh? Oh . . . me, I guess."

Rowan rolled a smoke. "Get me a beer, Andy," he said.

"Sure. Sure." Andy drew the beer and shuffled down behind the bar. A low murmur of voices came from the back hall of the big saloon.

Rowan sipped his beer. "Amos here?"

"Yeah. But he's busy, Rowan."

Rowan glanced at the back of the room. There was something bothering Andy. "Guess

I'll say a few words to him," said Rowan.

Andy swallowed. "Like I said – he's busy."

A door banged. Rowan clearly heard Hardtack's voice, then a yell of pain, and the door slammed. Rowan shoved the beer glass back. "I guess he is busy," he said quietly. He started for the back hall.

"Don't you go in there, Rowan! You ain't got the right to interfere with Mr. Darby's business!"

"Shut up, Andy," barked Rowan across his shoulder.

Rowan strode to the rear of the saloon and opened the door into the rear hallway.

"Oh, my God! said Andy.

Rowan gripped the doorknob of Darby's office and jerked the door open. Hardtack was standing in a corner. Dan Lacey was leaning against the wall, eying the old man, and Amos Darby was sitting on the edge of his big desk. He swiveled on his broad rump as Rowan came in. "What the hell you want?" he demanded.

Darby had always reminded Rowan of a fat fish. His green eyes had the inhuman coldness of a shark's. Rowan glanced at Hardtack. "What's the trouble, Hardtack?" he asked.

The old man glanced quickly at Lacey. "Nothin', Rowan. Nothin' at all."

Lacey straightened up. His face was set and

pale. "Get out of here, Emmett," he said thinly.

Rowan grinned. "Official business again, Lacey?"

Darby stood up. "This is private business, Emmett. You ain't wanted in here."

"I wasn't wanted in your hotel, Darby, but I'm still there."

"Yeah. Yeah. I heard about what you said to Seb Steffens, my clerk."

"So?"

"I run a respectable hotel and saloon," Darby said quietly. "You aim to stay in Silver Rock you better remember that!"

Rowan scratched his jaw. "Yeah. You've changed a lot since Tombstone and Sonora. When I was down there, I heard the Rurales are still interested in you."

Darby flushed. He glanced at Lacey. "You aim to let him talk like that? Slander, it is!"

Lacey was boiling beneath his cold expression. Rowan motioned to Hardtack. "Come on," he said.

"He'll get fired," warned Darby.

Rowan smiled. "I'm hiring the old vinegarroon. God knows I should know better, but he's working with me now."

Hardtack shuffled across the room. He got behind Rowan and sidled through the doorway. Rowan eyed both men. "I'm getting tired of the tactics in this town," he said. "Damned tired!" He backed out the door and grabbed Hardtack by the arm. He pushed him into the saloon. Hardtack headed for the bar, but Rowan steered him to the door and walked up the street. "What was that all about?" he asked.

Hardtack spat. "Darby wanted to know what we was doing out in the hills."

"You tell him?"

"You damned idjit! What do you take me for?"

Rowan glanced back. Lacey was standing on the porch of the Territorial, watching them. "Thanks," Rowan said to Hardtack, "for keeping your mouth shut."

"Wasn't easy for me. When does my pay start? I'll settle for a bottle of rye right now."

Rowan cursed. "You'll stay sober! We're going out there again tonight. You'll stay with me until we do!"

Hardtack rolled his eyes upward. "From one hellion of a boss to another. Ain't there no peace in this world?"

Rowan grinned. "All right. I'll buy you a double at the Yucca. That's as far as I'll go!"

CHAPTER EIGHT

Clouds gathered over Silver Hills late in the afternoon. By nightfall a cold wind was searching through the dusty streets and rattling windows. Rowan ate dinner and came up to his room after eight o'clock. Hardtack was fast asleep on Rowan's bed. Archer Lang was seated, reading, in his big armchair. He looked up at Rowan. "You strained our friendship today, Rowan," he said. He jerked a thumb at the sleeping prospector. "He's sawed at least a cord of wood in the last two hours. Makes almost as much noise asleep as he does awake."

Rowan took off his town clothes and replaced them with the rough trail clothing he had worn on his trip from Sonora. Lang lit a cigar. "You leaving town?" he asked.

Rowan swung his gun belt about his lean waist and buckled it. He took out his Colt and twirled the cylinder. "No. Hardtack and I are going to try to find the place where he lost his tools the night of the hold-up."

"Tools?"

Rowan swiftly explained Hardtack's story and the story of the mysterious drygulcher who had fired on them while they looked for the place. Archer stood up. "Then I'm going with you," he said.

Rowan grinned. He looked at Archer's slim white hands. "You don't aim to dig with those hands, do you?"

"Hell no! But at least I can keep guard for you, Rowan. I can shoot with these lilywhites, you know."

"Damned right you can. Thanks, *amigo*. I didn't want to ask you for help."

Lang began to change his clothing. "You *need* help, Rowan. By God, you haven't changed too much."

"What do you mean by that?"

"With the exception of Larry Farber, you always were a lone wolf. The way you've made bitter enemies about town is a caution. Beat up Durango. Rile Walt Sharpe. Threaten Dan Lacey and Amos Darby. You need a gambler's head to help you along."

Rowan sat down at the table and lit a cigar. He helped himself to the decanter. Lang buckled on his gun belt and slid a derringer into his coat pocket. "Wake up that old reprobate," he said. "I'll watch the whisky."

An hour later they left the livery stable and headed for the Creek Road. Rowan had picked up spades and picks. Hardtack was in a sour mood, but at least he was sober. They rode up the dry wash and Archer Lang took the horses, picketing them in a draw. He faded into the cold darkness to stand guard.

Hardtack quested back and forth like a mangy old hound wearing a battered hat. Rowan felt a tenseness grow in him. Up and down the wash the old man worked, probing now and then into the brush, coming out to scan his landmarks and then diving out of sight again as though looking for a long-forgotten bone. Then he came out again. "*Hist!* Rowan! I've found the place!"

Rowan forced his way through the brush. Hardtack was digging at the loose earth. He held up a rusted pick and then a shovel. He quested about and then held up an old Sharps rifle. Hardtack threw them down and slid down the bank. He walked slowly up the bed of the wash until he stood opposite a high bank of earth which rose higher to meet the lower slopes of the hills to the west. "This'll do," he said.

Rowan brought up the tools. Hardtack took a pick and set to work. For all Hardtack's age and dissipation, Rowan found it work to keep up with him. The old man burrowed deeper and deeper, working with the intentness of a dog trying to dig out a gopher. The wind grew colder. There was a trace of dampness in the air. The sweat dripped from Rowan's face, but he kept on. In an hour they were deep into the bank. Surprisingly enough, the earth was fairly easy to work. As though in answer to Rowan's thought, the old man turned, dashing the sweat from his face. "This dirt been moved before, Rowan. Woulda been hell diggin' through untouched soil."

Rowan shrugged. He set to and worked steadily. Another hour passed. Rowan threw down his shovel. "Christ, Hardtack," he said, "we've dug damned near through to the main shaft by now!"

Hardtack leaned on his shovel. "You tirin' out?" he jeered. "Don't make digging men like the *old* days. I'da thought after all them years in Yuma you coulda dug your way through the Rock of Gibraltar."

Rowan sat on a rock. Hardtack rolled a smoke. "This is the place, I tell yuh!"

"We'll dig clear to China," said Rowan in disgust.

Hardtack spat and set to work. "Sit there!" he jeered. "I'm part prairie dog and part mole. I'll show yuh!"

"You're part prairie dog, part mole and *all* loco, old man," said Rowan as he lit a smoke.

Hardtack struck hard. Earth fell. There was a faint rushing noise as earth slid down a slope. A breath of air, different from the cold wind, crept to Rowan. "See," said Hardtack, shoving his arm into the hole, "we've broke through into something."

Rowan snatched up his shovel and helped widen the hole. Hardtack slid down into the hole and was gone for a few minutes. Rowan could see the glow of his matches as he poked about. Hardtack poked his head out of the hole like a wise old gopher. "A drift," he said. "The props are still sound. Need a lantern now."

"There's one on my horse," said Rowan excitedly. "I'll get it." He scrambled up out of the hole.

A shot split the quiet. Rowan hit the dirt. He worked his way on hands and knees to the edge of the wash. The beating of hoofs came to him. Hardtack came up behind him. "What the hell was that?" he demanded.

Rowan stood up and looked to the east. The desert was still dark but the moon showed signs of breaking through the overcast. "I don't know, but we'd better find out." He drew his Colt and crossed the wash, Hardtack close behind. The moon broke through the clouds. A hundred yards from the edge of the wash there was a dark shadow beneath a mesquite bush. Rowan cocked his Colt and padded forward. A man was lying there. For one awful moment Rowan thought it might be

Archer, until he realized the man was much shorter and stockier. Rowan rolled him over. The moon shone on the sightless eyes of Denny Ellis. A bluish hole in the center of his eyes oozed blood and gray matter.

"For Christ's sake," muttered Hardtack.

Rowan looked about. There was no sign of Archer Lang. "We'd better pull tail out of here," he said. "We'll conceal the hole. I don't like this."

They went back to the hole and pulled brush over it. When they were done a man would have to fall into it to find it. They swung up on their horses and rode to the creek road, turning their heads constantly, hands gripping their Colts.

Archer Lang was in his room changing his clothes when Rowan came back to the hotel. He shook his head as Rowan entered the room. "My horse strayed. I followed him all the way to the road and then chased him damned near to town. How'd you make out?"

Rowan shoved back his hat. "We found the drift. At least I *think* we did. Who shot Ellis?"

Lang looked up in surprise. "Ellis? When did he get shot?"

Rowan poured a drink. "We heard a shot. Looked for you and found Denny Ellis with a hole in his forehead."

"Well, I'll be damned! Who did it?"

109

Rowan shrugged "Why didn't you come back?"

"Durango saw me come back into town. He was watching me. I figured I'd better stay here rather than have him follow me."

"You did right. Where are you going now?"

Lang waved a hand. "Back to my game. My luck has been good the last few nights."

Rowan dropped into the chair. "I'll see you later. You want to report Ellis' death?"

Lang shook his head. "Let him lie. They won't miss him much in Silver Rock."

Rowan sat for a long time thinking. He had been accused of two murders he hadn't committed and had paid for it with ten years of his life. He didn't want to be blamed for Ellis' death too. Rowan changed into his town clothes and slid the Colt beneath his waistband. He left the hotel and stopped in front of it. The moon had given up its futile fight with the clouds. The cold wind searched the streets, bringing the odor of rain with it. Rowan, on an impulse, walked to the Territorial. He pushed through the batwings and sat down near Lang's table. Half an hour drifted past. Boots thudded on the porch and Durango came in. He glanced at Rowan and went into the saloon office. In a few minutes Walt Sharpe appeared, followed by Amos Darby. They stopped at the end of the bar.

Dan Lacey joined them from the lookout seat. Lang glanced at Rowan. "Something's up," he said out of the side of his mouth.

Rowan shifted in his seat. Dan Lacey walked between the crowded tables and stopped in front of Rowan. "I want to talk with you," he said.

"Start talking."

"Where were you earlier this evening?"

Rowan looked past the marshal. Trevor Paine raised his head from where he sat at a nearby table. "Why?" asked Rowan.

"Official business."

"I went for a ride."

The soft slap of cards stopped. Conversation died away. Everyone looked at Rowan.

"Where?" asked Lacey.

"East of town."

Lacey nodded. "On the Creek Road?"

Rowan was irritated. "Yes!"

"Take it easy," advised Archer Lang.

Darby, Sharpe and Paine gathered behind Lacey. Durango had disappeared. Lacey rested his hand on his Colt. "You were out there quite a while, weren't you?"

"I might have been."

"What were you doing out there?"

"None of your damned business!" Rowan stood up.

111

Lacey smiled thinly. "You don't *have* to talk," he said. "We've got something to show you."

The batwings pushed open. Durango was bent beneath the weight of a body. He dumped Denny Ellis on a table. The men standing near it drew back. "It's Ellis," one of them said, "with a hole in his skull!"

Rowan eyed the crowd. "I didn't kill him," he said, "if that's what everyone is thinking."

"You've killed before," said Sharpe.

"You *were* out there, weren't you?" asked Darby.

Durango came close to Lacey. "I was out there looking for Denny," he said quietly. "I saw Emmett leave the wash. Later I found Denny's body up the wash. His guns hadn't been fired."

"Well?" asked Lacey.

Rowan shifted a little. This was something he hadn't foreseen. He glanced at Archer Lang. The gambler was sliding his cards from one supple hand to the other. "I was out there," said Rowan, "but I didn't kill Ellis."

Trevor Paine grunted. "You didn't kill Farber and Ganoe either, did you, Emmett? That's what you always claimed."

The crowd moved closer. The batwings swung open. Hardtack came in, glanced at Ellis and then at Rowan. He spoke softly

112

to Andy. The barkeeper was evidently explaining what was happening. Hardtack nodded and asked for a double rye.

"You'd better lock him up, Lacey," said Paine, "until we get to the bottom of this."

Hardtack wiped his mouth. "I'll get you to the bottom," he said loudly.

The crowd turned to look at Hardtack. "Give me another double," said Hardtack to Andy. "Might be a while before I get another."

"Shut the old rumdum up," said Darby.

Hardtack downed his drink. "Darby," he said quietly, "I always wanted to say this when I worked for you but never had the guts at the time. Of all the fat, fourflushing, tinhorn, backstabbing, crooked —"

"Shut up, damn you!" yelled Darby.

Lacey turned on a heel and started for Hardtack. "Wait," said Rowan. "Let him alone, Lacey!"

Lacey turned and tested Rowan with his eyes. Rowan smiled. "Try *me*, Lacey," he said, "if you've got the guts."

Hardtack pushed through the crowd. "I killed Ellis," he said, "if that's what you want."

"The old bastard is drunk!" said Sharpe.

Hardtack spat at Sharpe's feet. "I said I did it, didn't I? Or would you rather have Rowan say he did it? Yeah. That's it! Well, let him alone, I did it!"

"Lock him up," said Paine quietly. His cold eyes met Rowan's and did not waver.

Lacey went to Hardtack and took him by the arm. The old man pulled his arm away. "I can go to the *jazgado* under my own power," he said. "I been there before and never had any help. See you gents later!"

The crowd went back to their drinking and gambling. Darby and Sharpe went into Darby's office. Durango went to the lookout seat. Lang spoke quietly to Rowan. "That was a close one. What are you going to do now?"

Rowan rolled a smoke. "Get that damned fool out of the *calabozo*."

"That might not be easy."

Rowan eyed his friend. "Nothing is easy in Silver Rock, Archer. *Nothing*."

Rowan left the Territorial and walked up the street to the jail. Lacey was leaving the building. He passed Rowan without a word. Rowan went into the marshal's office and asked Sam Corbett if he could see Hardtack. The deputy waved him on. Hardtack was lying on his bunk, puffing clouds of smoke at the ceiling. He grinned as he saw Rowan. "Home is where the heart is," he said. "Maybe I'll retire here."

"Why the hell did you do it, Hardtack?"

Hardtack sat up. "Look, sonny! They woulda jugged you proper if it hadn't been for me. I'll take the blame for the killin' to let you be free to work. It's best this way, Rowan."

Rowan shook his head. "You've been a great friend, Hardtack."

"Shut up! Dammit! Now you get movin'. You find that damned bullion and clear yourself, and then get me outta here afore they string me up."

Rowan nodded. "Okay, I'll do my best. Anything I can do for you?"

Hardtack closed one faded eye. "You know damned well what you can do."

"Get Angie?"

"Damn you! You know what I mean."

Rowan left the jail and bought a bottle at the Yucca. He walked down the side alley, next to the jail, and tapped on the bars. A thin hand thrust out between the bars and closed on the bottle with a viselike grip. The bottle vanished. Rowan grinned and walked up to Bonanza Street. Getting Hardtack out of the jail was another problem to be solved. Time was running short. Rowan had a feeling, as he walked to the hotel, that the showdown was getting closer.

CHAPTER NINE

In the days when Silver Rock had been a boom town, the discovery of a body with a hole between its eyes would have caused a short period of excitement, unless it had been the body of a top gun, a lawman or an ace gambler. The deaths of men like Denny Ellis, satellites of more important men, never had mattered much except to fan the flames of the bitter feuds that existed between bigger men fighting for power. But now, the publicly unmourned death of Denny Ellis, a pawn in the dark struggle for fifty thousand dollars in silver bullion, seemed to draw wire-tight the tension that had been steadily developing in shabby Silver Rock.

The tension was obvious in the saloons. The usual noisy card games, which were played during daylight hours for small stakes by men who had no visible means of support, now became quiet, with the players eying each man who came into the bar. The general store, always a beehive of gossiping women and lounging men, now became an information center on the latest signs or movements of the principals in the quiet struggle.

116

The second morning after the arrest of Hardtack, Rowan did the town, as he had done in the old days as marshal. He walked from the hotel, at Second and Bonanza, to the intersection of First and Bonanza, where the Silver Nugget and the Territorial Bar faced each other across the main street. It was a cloudless day, with a bright sun, but a cold wind still swept through the quiet streets. Rowan stopped outside the Silver Nugget and lit a cigar. Across First Street, facing each other across Bonanza, were the two empty shells that had once been saloons such as the Territorial and the Silver Nugget. The burned-out Road To Ruin and the sagging Taj Mahal. Rowan thought back on the days when all four saloons had been open twenty-four hours a day, and all of them doing a land office business. In those days it took speed and dexterity to get across either First or Bonanza because of the traffic of cowboys racing their horses; freight wagons, grinding through the yellow dust; ore wagons groaning under their heavy loads; Concord coaches swaying on their leather thoroughbraces; a tired troop of cavalry, masked with alkali dust, trotting through town on their never-ending search for the elusive Apaches.

Now the intersection dreamed in the cold sun. Now and then a woman hurried by on a shopping trip. Here and there a hipshot pony stood at a hitching rack. A Mexican belabored a shaggy burro, laden high with faggots, right down the center of Bonanza. It was so damned quiet it was hard to believe. Rowan shook his head and walked slowly to the east, his boots echoing hollowly on the boardwalks. Down Bonanza to Mesquite, where Bengson's General Store faced the shabby Barrel House across Bonanza. Across Mesquite was the Yucca Saloon, and next door to that was the office of the newspaper. Rowan felt an impulse to stop by the office, but the memory of Ellen's bitter words the last time they had spoken with each other was too vivid for Rowan. He went into the Yucca.

Jim Bond was at the bar, having a morning pick-me-up. He motioned Rowan to the bar beside him and shoved over the bottle. "Bad habit of mine, Rowan," he said with a smile. "Double shot before business hours. Gives me the strength to face this town."

Rowan filled his glass. "I know what you mean," he said. "But why do you stay?"

Jim shrugged. "I like it here."

"There's no accounting for tastes," Rowan said dryly.

Jim turned to look squarely at Rowan. "Don't you?"

"I used to."

"Why?"

"It was lively then. I was a lot younger. I had a good job."

"So, if you clear yourself, you'll pull out of here forever?"

Rowan nodded.

Jim sipped his drink. "I wish it wasn't so."

"You're still crusading, Jim. You'll crusade until someone puts a slug through you. I've seen it happen before."

Jim shook his head. "No. Look here. I've done a lot of work on my own regarding Silver Rock. It's a natural trading center for miners, ranchers and farmers. The roads are good between here and other towns. The railroad would consider a branch line if the area developed sufficiently. The climate is excellent. There's plenty of water."

Rowan shrugged. "You're forgetting the main obstacle, Jim. It's a nest of skunks."

Jim laughed. "I'll have to agree to that. But that's part of the growing pains of every town. Their day comes and goes. The days of the honest, hardworking citizen comes and *stays*. That's the difference."

"Jim, I hate to say this, but I'm in no mood to contemplate the civic future of Silver Rock."

Bond placed a hand on Rowan's shoulder. "I've been doing a lot of thinking, Rowan.

119

More or less hand-picking the men I think will help make Silver Rock a town of the future. You're one of them."

"I won't be here long enough to enjoy the future of Silver Rock."

"Bitter. Bitter," said Jim quietly. He refilled his glass. "You're an unusual man, Rowan. As I understand, you had very little education before you went to Yuma. Yet you speak as though you had better schooling than your record shows."

Rowan laughed harshly. "I read every book I could get my hands on in Yuma. One of my cellmates was a former professor in an Eastern college. It helped pass his time and mine to teach me as much as he could."

"Why did you do it?"

"Dammit! To pass the time!"

Bond waggled a hand. "You're wrong. Whether you knew it or not you were preparing yourself for a useful life."

"In Silver Rock, I suppose?"

"Not necessarily. Anywhere. But you *did* come back to Silver Rock."

Rowan drained his glass. "You know why I came back."

"I must say that you've handled yourself well, Rowan. No shooting. But how long do you think this situation will continue? There's a feeling of tension in this town. They tried to get you back in a cell night before last and failed because you had one loyal friend in town."

Rowan looked quickly at the newspaperman. "You know damned well Hardtack didn't kill Ellis."

"Yes. And you didn't either. But Hardtack put himself in jeopardy to leave you free to work out your destiny."

Rowan raised his hat. "Your eloquence pleases my uncultured ears," he said.

Jim shoved the bottle back. *"Gracias!* I want you to know one thing, Rowan – you served your time in Yuma. You may feel as though everyone in Silver Rock is against you. You're not alone. Many people here are with you rather than with Sharpe and Darby. Somehow I have a feeling that the future of this town depends on what happens in this involved situation."

Rowan gripped the man's shoulder. "Thanks, Jim."

Bond turned to go. "Another thing – you havedn't seen Ellen of late – to speak with her, that is," he said quietly.

Rowan turned from the bar. "Let's forget that kind of talk, Jim. You've left me with a good feeling. Don't spoil it!"

Bond shrugged and left the bar. Rowan reached for the bottle and then shoved it back. He turned on a heel and went out.

Rowan went to the livery stable and got Smoky. He rode to the west of town, letting the roan full out once he was past the last pitiful shacks of the town. He followed the course of the creek, riding mile after mile, enjoying the full sweep of the cold wind. The distant mountains stood out sharply against the sky for a change, instead of being robed in dim purple haze. A roadrunner scuttled ahead of Smoky with its odd stride. A ragged buzzard hovered high overhead on motionless wings, drifting with an updraft. It was a good country, Rowan thought. Too damned good for men like Sharpe and Darby. Maybe Jim Bond, for all his small-time crusading, was right.

Rowan rode most of the day, lunching at a small ranch on the Clearwater. Two tousle-headed kids played with him for a time. The stocky, likeable rancher showed Rowan where he had dammed a fork of the creek to make a waterhole for the dry days. He was proud of his new Chicago windmill that banged and rattled in the strong wind. His house was snug, his barn well filled. His small herd dotted a distant slope. When Rowan left he took with him a verbal invitation to come again, any time, and have dinner. He stopped Smoky on a ridge and looked back.

The rancher waved from his doorway.

In the late afternoon Rowan rode back toward Silver Rock. The roan was tired, but Rowan had learned that the prophetic words of Jim Bond held a ring of truth in them. The country, once almost empty of life ten years before, was now dotted with small ranches, farms which huddled in the rich bottomlands, small mines which would never pour a stream of wealth into the hands of the men who worked them, but which promised to be steady moneymakers. Jim was right. Silver Rock had the advantage of position. It had a future.

Rowan bought two dinners in the Busy Bee and had them placed in a hamper. He bought a bottle of rye, supplemented it with several bottles of beer, and then made his way to the *calabozo*. Sam Corbett, engrossed in carving a chain from a single piece of wood, waved Rowan on to the cell row, tossing him the key.

Hardtack was whistling the *Sago Lily* when Rowan appeared. The old man licked his lips as Rowan spread the dinner out on the small table in the cell. "Where's the bottle I gave you night before last?" Rowan demanded.

Hardtack tilted his head. "Damned cold in here, *amigo*. My tubes was clogged."

Rowan shook his head. "Dig in," he said, opening two bottles of beer.

123

Hardtack ate voraciously. When he was done he drained a second bottle of beer. *"Bueno!"* he said. "I'm beginning to feel as though I might live in this drafty hole."

"You'll outlive me, you old goat."

Hardtack spat. "Give me a smoke," he said. "Where you heading after you leave here?"

"Back to that drift."

"Alone?"

"I'm going to ask Arch to go with me."

"Bueno. He's a good man. Watch for holes in there."

Rowan lit a cigar. "I'll get you out of here as quickly as I can."

Hardtack waved a hand. "It ain't bad. Howsomever, I'm itchin' to get out. Maybe you should ought to wait until I *do* get out. I know them drifts better'n any man hereabouts, Rowan."

Rowan shook his head. "No time. Thanks anyway, Hardtack." He took the bottle from where he had hidden it in the bottom of the hamper and placed it on the table. "Happy days," he said and left the cell, locking it behind him. The pop of the cork followed the clicking of the key.

Arch Lang was in his room. He listened to what Rowan had to say. "Yes," he said quietly, "I'll go along. I won't rest until this

124

mess is cleared up. The sooner the better."

The clouds had filled the sky again that night. It was late when Rowan and Archer reached the wash. Archer took the horses and Rowan slid down into the hole Hardtack and he had dug into the drift. He had a small pick and a light shovel. He lit the lantern and felt his way down into the old tunnel.

The yellow light of the lantern cast dancing shadows in the dark tunnel. The pit props were sound enough although here and there one of them sagged. Piles of sifted earth showed on the floor of the drift. He counted his steps as he went slowly in. Now and then he stopped, hearing only the distant drip of water. After two hundred steps he stopped and lit a cigar. The air was cold and damp. He picked up the lantern and went on. Suddenly, behind him, he heard a rustling noise. He turned swiftly, stepping behind a prop before he realized it was the rush of a fall of earth. He turned and stepped forward, and his foot met nothing. He fell forward with a yell, thrusting out his hands. The lantern dropped from his hand. His left hand gripped a projecting prop, and he smashed against it, scrabbling desperately with his right hand for a hold. His fingers seemed to bite into the wood, and he hung there, swinging back and forth. He risked a glance downward. The lantern had fallen on a ledge fifty feet below. The yellow light still flooded out.

Rowan swallowed hard. He worked his right elbow up on the prop and hung there, breathing hard. Slowly he extended his left hand and gripped the base of a vertical prop. He inched his way forward until he could rest his left forearm on the lip of the hole and then worked his way up, stabbing his boot toes into the damp earth. The loose earth pattered down. Far below him he could hear the splash of water as the dirt struck a pool. Cold sweat flowed down his sides. With a desperate heave he threw his left leg up on the brink, gripped hard with his left hand and pulled himself forward and then heaved himself over the edge, rolling a good ten feet away from the pit.

He lay face downward on the damp earth, his heart thudding against his ribs. It had been too damned close for comfort. He sat up and lit a cigar. He had stowed several candles in his coat pocket, and he drew one out and lit it. It was a good twenty minutes before he could go back and look down into the pit. He raised the candle. The tunnel beyond the pit was blocked by a fall of earth. There was no way to get across. He shrugged and started back.

His right foot kicked something against a prop. He lowered the candle. A pistol lay on the floor. He squatted over it and picked it up. There was no mistaking the long thin barrel and the rounded bird's-head butt, as different from a Colt Frontier as a Sharps is from a Winchester rifle. It was a Colt Lightning. Rowan didn't have to hold it close to the candle to know whose it was. The initials carved into the ivory butt plates were plain enough. L.R.F. "Lawrence Reid Farber," said Rowan aloud.

He squatted there for a long time handling the rusted handgun. Larry must have been brought in here. The body must have been hidden in the drift, possibly in the pit Rowan had almost fallen into. The revolver might have been dropped from the holster as the body was carried into the drift, and then been overlooked by the killers. Rowan stood up and slid the familiar gun beneath his waistband. He walked back to the entrance and scrambled out. A spit of rain hit his face as he concealed the hole.

Archer Lang met him in the wash. "Well?" he asked.

Rowan drew out the Colt Lightning. "Larry's," he said quietly.

Lang looked quickly at the gun and then at Rowan. "Did you find the body?"

127

"No. The way is blocked."

"You think it's in there?"

"Yes."

"What about the bullion?"

Rowan shrugged. "I didn't expect to find it this easy. I'm not sure it's even in there. But I've got a lead on Larry's death."

"What will you do with the pistol?"

"I'm going to show it to Jim Bond. Jim is on my side. He's a good man to have with you. He never believed I killed Larry Farber and Mike Ganoe."

"*Bueno!* Let's get back to town. It's going to rain like hell tonight."

They turned up their collars as the rain began to sift down, and rode toward the road. Rowan touched the butt of the rusted gun beneath his waistband. For the first time since he had returned to Silver Rock he had a feeling that he might be on the trail to clearing himself.

CHAPTER TEN

The morning after Rowan found the gun he left the room and ate in the Busy Bee. He'd have to enter the mine through the old heading now. There was no way of telling how far the earth fall in the old drift extended. But there was only one man he could trust who knew the mine drifts. Hardtack. Until he got the old man out of the *jazgado* he was stymied. He went back to his room. Archer Lang was gone. Rowan went to his dresser and looked for the Colt Lightning. It was gone. Desperately he searched the room, and then he went downstairs. The relief clerk was polishing the lamp globes. "Where's Arch Lang?" asked Rowan.

"Went out right after you did."

"Anyone go upstairs this morning?"

The clerk looked queerly at Rowan. "Hell, yes! We've got maids in this hotel, although you'd never know it to look at it."

"I mean anyone else?"

"Half a dozen people staying here. Why?"

Rowan waved a hand and left the hotel. He had planned to show the weapon to Jim Bond. Archer Lang was eating breakfast in the Western Star. Rowan asked him about the gun.

Lang finished his coffee. "I left right after you did."

"See anyone in the halls?"

Lang nodded. "Walt Sharpe," he said. "Durango was with him."

Rowan smacked a fist into his other palm.

Lang lit a cigar. "No use asking *them,* is there?" he asked.

Rowan shook his head. "Anyway, you can swear that you saw it."

"Certainly. But what will it prove?"

"Nothing alone. Coupled with other information it may mean a lot. Keep your mouth shut about it."

"You know me well enough to know I don't talk, Rowan," said Lang with a smile.

Rowan left the restaurant and hurried to the newspaper office. Jim Bond and Ellen were at work. Ellen nodded, but did not speak. Jim listened as Rowan told him of the gun.

Bond slapped his hand down on his desk when the story was through. "It's a lead," he said. "You're sure there's no way to get farther into that drift?"

"It looked like a solid fall. Might take days to get through it, and I couldn't do it alone."

Bond nodded. "Then you'll have to go through the mine heading. Damned dangerous business, Rowan."

Rowan smiled. "Everything I've done since I've come here has been dangerous."

Rowan glanced at Ellen. "Thank God you've got a lead anyway, slim as it is."

Rowan walked to the door. "I'll see you later."

Ellen raised her head as Rowan closed the door. There was a look of pain in her eyes.

Rowan went past the jail and told Hardtack what had happened. The old man bobbed his head. "We was *right*, then! They must have taken Farber in there. By God, Rowan, I got to get out of here to give you a hand! You ain't going down into the heading without me."

"I might have to."

"Maybe you can spring me, Rowan."

Rowan shook his head. "Too risky. I can't get over the line between order and breaking the law. One slip and I'll be in here with you."

"Yeah," said Hardtack gloomily.

"Take it easy, old-timer, I'll see what I can do."

Rowan went to his room. He wanted time to think. Footsteps sounded in the hall and someone rapped at the door. "Come in," Rowan called.

The door opened and the lean hawk face of Trevor Paine looked in. Paine shut the door behind him. "Emmett, he said, "I've just talked with Jim Bond."

"So?"

Paine came farther into the room and sat down. "He told me about the gun you found."

Rowan cursed mentally. Damn Bond and his big mouth.

Paine lifted a slim white hand. "I know what you're thinking. You've always felt as though I was allied with Sharpe, Darby and their ilk."

"Well?"

"In your anger at being sent to Yuma you lashed out at everyone. I'll admit I handled that case well, shaving points a bit close, but all of it was legal, Emmett."

"You did a fine job, Paine."

Paine's dark eyes studied Rowan. "I'm a good lawyer, Emmett. I may have my faults, as we all do, but I know my profession."

"You didn't come here to tell me how good you are."

"No. I came here because I want to help you."

Rowan felt as though he had been slapped hard across the mouth.

Paine reached for the bottle on the table and poured a drink. "At the time of the trial I was as sure of your guilt as I am that I'm sitting here right now. I paid little attention to the case after you were sentenced. When you came back I hated the sight of you, because I thought you should have been hung. The recent events, in which you've played a leading role, have bothered me. You're a bullheaded, antagonistic man, Emmett, but the very way you've carried yourself lately brought some doubts into my mind. The finding of Farber's gun has solidified some of those doubts. I want to help you."

Rowan filled a glass. "It's almost too late, isn't it?"

"No. You've lost ten years of your life. For that I'm sorry, now that I'm beginning to doubt your guilt. But it's too late to go back. You're still a young man with a future. I'd like to see you clear yourself."

"Thanks. I'm doing all right playing a lone hand."

Paine lifted his glass. "*No* man plays a lone hand in this life, Emmett."

Boots thudded against the floor of the hall. A hand hammered against the door. "Who is it?" called Rowan.

"Andy, the barkeep! Archer Lang just shot Amos Darby to death! He wants you to come over!"

Rowan jumped to his feet. Trevor Paine stood up. "It doesn't surprise me," he said. "There has been bad blood between those two for years."

Rowan hurried down the stairs and up the long block to the Territorial. Women stood on the boardwalk, looking through the dusty windows. Rowan pushed through the batwings. Arch Lang sat at his usual table. He nodded as Rowan came in. The place was crowded with men. A body lay on the floor, concealed by a cover from a pool table. Dan Lacey was at the bar, talking with Walt Sharpe. Archer Lang's Colt lay on the table. Rowan sat down next to his friend. "What happened?"

Archer's dark eyes flicked toward the body. "That tinhorn owed me money. I came in to collect. He offered to cut the cards, double or nothing. I won the first cut and he wanted two out of three. He took the second cut. I took the third. He called me a cheat. I slapped his face. He drew. I killed him. Keno!"

Rowan eyed Lacey. "What about him?"

Lang laughed shortly. "Half a dozen men were watching us. They saw what happened. Self-defense, Rowan."

"Why did you want me?"

Lang looked about the crowded room. "Thought I might have trouble getting out of here."

Lacey came across the room and looked at Lang. "I can't hold you," he said, "but I won't forget this, Lang. Amos didn't have a chance against you."

Lang yawned and stood up. He slid his Colt into its holster. "Evidently *he* thought he did." He looked at Rowan. "Come on. I need a drink." He dusted off his coat and walked ahead of Rowan to the door.

"Slickest shooting I ever saw," a man said. "Amos had the drop on him. Lang fired almost as soon as his cutter cleared leather. Boots up for Darby."

"You take it damned cool," said Rowan to his friend as they walked toward the Yucca.

Archer Lang turned his head slightly. "It was self-defense, as I said. It's to your advantage, Rowan. Darby was after your scalp."

"I don't like it, Arch."

"Why? You're in the clear."

Rowan shrugged. There was a cold, impersonal tone in Lang's voice.

Archer pushed open one of the batwings and stood aside to let Rowan pass. "It's the way the cards fall, Rowan," he said softly.

Talk was still rife in the town that evening when Rowan went up to his room. Lang had coolly moved his base of operations to the Silver Nugget, directly across the street from the Territorial Bar, and was now busy at his work, playing cards with long, slim hands. Rowan dropped on his bed and placed his hands behind his head. Archer Lang was a product of his environment. Yet something had left the Archer Lang Rowan had remembered. He was as warmhearted and courteous as ever, but his hot courage of ten years ago had settled into a cold deadliness. Rowan

135

remembered the day he had shot Denny Ellis through the arm when Durango and Ellis had tried to maul Rowan. It would have been just as easy for Lang to kill Ellis as it had been to cripple him. Rowan couldn't help wondering why he hadn't done the same to Amos Darby.

There was a light rap on the door. "Come in," said Rowan without getting up.

The door opened and Ellen Farber stood there, with the low lamplight bringing out the color of her hair. Rowan's feet hit the floor with a crash. "I'm sorry," he said, "I didn't expect a lady."

She smiled. "I *hope* not," she said. "May I sit down?"

Rowan cleared a chair and placed it beside her. She sat down. "You may still be angry with me, Rowan," she said, "but you must overlook it for the time being."

"I've forgotten any difficulties we may have had."

She leaned forward. "I have been doing a lot of thinking since you told Jim about finding Larry's gun."

"Yes?"

"I've thought back to the days before the killings you were accused of. I remembered one night, shortly before the holdup, when some man came to see Larry. I was sleepy. They were talking in the living room. I didn't recognize the other man's voice, but I remembered one thing he said. It was this – 'Everything is set, Larry. You've got nothing to worry about if you play your part. What about Emmett?' "

Rowan came close to her. "So?"

"Larry assured the man that you would be taken care of. That was all."

"You can't remember who it was?"

She shook her head. "I was sleepy. I fell asleep and forgot about it. It wasn't until I began to think of events before the crime that it came back to me. Does it help?"

He rubbed his jaw. "It only seems to substantiate the story you told me about Larry. That is, that Larry might have had something to do with the crime. But there was nothing definite in what you told me." The words of Archer Lang came back to him – maybe Larry was mixed up in the robbery. Those had been his words, and Archer was a man with more insight than most men.

Rowan looked down at the serious woman. "Thanks," he said. "I was a fool to ride you roughshod the way I did. I'm not the polished type, Ellen."

She stood up. "I feel as though you'll solve this thing. But be careful. You're walking an awfully thin wire, Rowan."

On an impulse Rowan drew her close. She

rested her head on his chest. "I've been more lonely the last few days than I have been in the last ten years."

He kissed her, and she clung to him with a passion that aroused him. He bent her back and kissed her throat. "Please," she said. "Rowan . . ."

Someone walked up the hall and stopped outside the door. Rowan released her, and she stepped back and touched her hair. Rowan opened the door. A strange cowpoke was in the hall, looking up at the room number. "You Rowan Emmett?" he asked.

"Yes."

"Cassie Whitlow wants to see yuh. Says it's important." The cowpoke saw Ellen and lifted his eyebrows.

"Thanks," said Rowan. He closed the door.

Ellen eyed him. "Are you going to see her?" she asked.

"Why not?"

She flushed. "She's no good, Rowan."

"Maybe. In some ways. But she was always a friend of mine. She probably doesn't want to see me just for pleasure, Ellen."

She opened the door. "Go then!"

Rowan listened to the quick tap of her feet against the floor of the hall. Then he grinned. "Spunky," he said aloud. "Rowan Emmett, you're in trouble again."

Rowan stopped in the Silver Nugget to see Archer Lang. His table was occupied by another gambler. Rowan left the saloon and walked to Mesquite Street. Durango was standing in front of the Barrel House on the corner of Mesquite and Bonanza. His cold eyes followed Rowan as he passed by. Rowan walked into Cassie's Castle, fended off one of the hurdy-gurdy girls, and walked into Cassie's office. She was seated at her desk, the combs askew in her golden hair. One shoulder of her black sheath gown had slipped, revealing the full upper curve of one of her breasts. Her head swayed a little as she looked at Rowan. "Shut the door," she said thickly. "I wanta talk with you."

Rowan shut the door and sat down. The place was foul with tobacco fumes, the odor of whisky and the strong perfume she wore.

"You ain't been around much," she said accusingly.

"You call me here to tell me *that?*"

"Damn you!"

Rowan got up.

Cassie sat up straight. "Sit down!" she ordered. "I got something to tell you."

"Shoot."

She poured two drinks and shoved one toward Rowan. "You been working hard trying to clear yourself," she said. "Looks like you're on the trail of something hot. Just wanted to warn you."

Rowan stood up and opened the window behind Cassie's desk. The cool night air blew in. The draft sucked some of the smoke and fumes from the little office.

"The deck was stacked against you ten years ago," she said. She drained her glass and reached for the decanter. "Damn! It's empty. Get a bottle, Rowan."

"You've had too much already."

She smiled slyly. "No bottle, no talk."

Rowan shrugged. He went to the door and called one of the bartenders. He turned to Cassie. "Well?"

She hiccuped. "There's a man in this burg who's been working undercover for years. Clever as sin. Knows as much about that robbery and those killings as God does. You know that?"

The bartender came into the hall. He stopped outside the door, and Rowan took the bottle from him. Cassie leaned forward. "I'm going to warn you, Rowan. Look out for –"

Suddenly a pistol crashed just behind her. Smoke swirled into the room from the open window. Cassie Whitlow slumped forward, scattering the empty glasses on her desk. Rowan shoved the barkeep aside and sprinted

140

down the hall. He threw open a back door and ran out into the alleyway. A gun split the quiet. The slug whined from an adobe wall inches from Rowan. He dropped flat, snaked out his Colt and fired without leveling it. There was a yelp of pain from a shadowy figure standing in Pitahaya Street and then the thud of boots hitting the hard earth. Rowan jumped to his feet and cocked his Colt. He ran to Pitahaya and turned west on the dark street. There was no one in sight.

Rowan went back to the saloon. Cassie was lying on the sofa in her office. Two of her girls were with her. The barkeep looked at Rowan with a pale, sweat-beaded face. "My God!" he said. "Who did it?"

Rowan shook his head and went to Cassie. The girls stood aside. "Too late," one of them said. "Right through the back. Ain't got long to live."

The powdered face had relaxed, and the reddened lips were parted. The combs had fallen from the dyed hair. Cassie opened her eyes. "You there . . . Rowan?" she asked huskily.

"Yes. Yes."

"Who . . . was it?"

"I don't know."

She closed her eyes. "You remember . . . the old . . . days. Rowan?"

"Yes."

"The . . . Golden Girl."

"Take it easy."

"No . . . it's just as . . . well. Rather . . . go while I got *some* . . . looks left."

Rowan bent close. "Who were you trying to tell me about?"

"Who? Oh . . . yeah." She tried to get up, but Rowan pressed her back.

"Doc is on the way," said one of the girls from the door.

Cassie gripped Rowan's sleeve. She opened her eyes. "You damned . . . idiot," she gasped. "Only . . . real man . . . I ever . . . knew."

She lay back. For a moment it seemed to Rowan that her earlier beauty had come back to grace her again. He covered her face with her scarf and turned to lower the light. He picked up one of her gray combs and put it into his pocket. He pushed his way through the silent people in the hallway and passed through the saloon. He felt as though another door in his past life had closed behind him forever.

CHAPTER ELEVEN

The day after Cassie Whitlow's death the whole town seemed to be idle. The body had been laid out in Pearce's Mortuary, and all day long the sympathetic and the curious paid their last respects to the Golden Girl. Lacey had questioned Rowan, only to find Rowan's story backed by Joe Keleher, the bartender who had been standing in the hallway when Cassie was shot. A messenger had gone after the sheriff, only to return with the information that the sheriff was in Tucson on business. Doc Lake had acted as coroner, rendering a verdict that Cassandra Whitlow had died from a bullet which had penetrated the lobar area. Arrangements had been made for the funeral.

Rowan left the funeral parlor to meet Hardtack Christie walking toward Pearce's. "How did you get out?" Rowan asked.

Hardtack grinned. "Trevor Paine got me out. Don't ask me how." He looked at the funeral parlor. "Who done it, Rowan?"

"I don't know. I may have winged the bastard, though."

Hardtack mopped his face. "She was all right," he said thickly. "A fine woman. Drank

143

too much, but hell – we all do." He shuffled forward. "Wait for me, Rowan."

Rowan stepped up on the walk and leaned against a store front. All morning he had been looking for a man who limped or who carried an arm stiffly, hoping to pin down the man who had killed Cassie Whitlow, but his luck was bad.

Trevor Paine stopped beside Rowan. "You can go ahead now," he said quietly. "I got Hardtack out. You may need him."

Rowan eyed the thin-faced lawyer. He had not fitted Paine into the plan of things. Was the lawyer angling for a cut of the lost bullion? If so, he was due for a sharp come-uppance. *"Gracias,"* said Rowan.

Paine looked at the people filing into the funeral parlor. "I'd like to know who did that," he said.

Rowan nodded. "She was all right," he said. "Always good for a loan or a free drink. I didn't think she had an enemy in town."

Paine adjusted his white cuffs. "Perhaps she knew too much," he suggested.

Rowan lit his cigar." Perhaps. I marked the man who did it, Paine. I'll settle with him when I find him."

"I'd like a piece of him myself." Paine tipped his hat to a lady passing by. "Watch *your* back, Rowan."

"I'm safe as long as the silver isn't found."

The dark eyes studied him. "And if it *is* found?"

Rowan puffed at his cigar. "I still can take care of myself."

"Yes," said the lawyer thoughtfully. "I'm sure you can." He passed along the walk.

Hardtack came from the parlor. There was a suspicious moistness in his faded eyes. "Beautiful," he said, "plumb lovely. A fine woman she was. Silver Rock will never be the same."

They walked to the hotel. Hardtack glanced at Rowan. "When do we go?" he asked.

"When we get a chance. I feel as though every man in town is watching us."

"You can just bet they are, sonny."

Ellen Farber was waiting for them in the hotel lobby. "Rowan," she said, "don't go down into that mine."

He smiled. "Who said I was?"

"I know you intend to."

Rowan looked about the deserted lobby. "A man has a trail to follow through his life," he said. "Sometimes it's easy. Sometimes he can't leave it, or go back. This is one of those times. There has been too much spent on this thing already. It has to be settled."

She bent her head. "All right. I knew it was useless.' She looked up again. "I'll

145

be waiting for you," she said. She left the lobby.

Hardtack came close to Rowan. "I'll get things ready," he said. "When do you want to leave?"

"Whenever we get a chance. Arch will help us."

"*Bueno!* See you later." The old man left the hotel.

Rowan went up to his room. Three of the characters in the deadly play had left the scene forever. Of the three – Denny Ellis, Cassie Whitlow and Amos Darby – only Darby's death was clear-cut. Rowan still had to contend with Walt Sharpe, Durango and probably Dan Lacey. Sharpe was the brains, and Durango and Lacey were two dangerous allies. Yet Rowan had the uncanny skill of Hardtack Christie on his side, coupled with the cool courage of straight-shooting Archer Lang. The odds were even, the stakes high. The game wouldn't have much time left to play out.

Archer Lang came in and placed a bottle on the table. He opened it and filled two glasses. There was a set look on his handsome face. He handed Rowan a glass.

"What's troubling you, *amigo?*" asked Rowan.

Lang downed his drink and refilled the

glass. "I was down to see Cassie," he said quietly.

"Hell of a thing, Arch."

"Yes. She was a real woman. Had more of a soul than some of the nose-in-the-air women about this stinking town."

Rowan looked quickly at him. He suddenly remembered the first day he had been in town, when he had mentioned Archer's name to Cassie.

Lang leaned back in his chair and closed his eyes. "I can tell you this, Rowan: She and I once were pretty close. It was a long time ago. After you left Silver Rock. I ran into her here and there throughout the west. Finally, we drifted apart forever."

"So?"

The dark eyes studied Rowan. "I never quite got her out of my system. She could have passed in any stratum of society with a little education and polish. She could have helped a man get ahead. It was the bottle that hurt Cassie. It was why we broke up long ago. I had plans for us – marry her, take her out of this hole. Get a place in St. Louis, Denver or Chicago and live like society. It wasn't to be."

"Why?"

Archer smiled thinly and looked down at his slim hands. "Money," he said. *"Lots* of money. We were spenders, Cassie and I.

Maybe it's just as well. We might have grown to hate each other."

Rowan drained his glass. "I thought you were carrying the torch for Ellen Farber."

"That was different. She isn't my type. Ellen wants a home and children. Cassie and I wanted bright lights and champagne."

Rowan nodded. It was a side of Archer Lang he had never known. "You'll give me a hand tonight, won't you?"

"You're going down into the heading?"

"Yes."

"What do you want me to do?"

"Watch for Sharpe, Durango and Lacey."

"You think they'll try to follow you?"

"Who else would?"

Lang nodded. "I'll help. I'll keep them busy. But, for God's sake, be careful down there! I don't want to lose you, Rowan. You're the only man I can truthfully say is my friend."

Rowan filled his glass and silently toasted the gambler.

The long hours drifted past. Rowan cleaned and reloaded his guns. Archer Lang left the room and scouted the town at Rowan's suggestion. It was well after dark when Hardtack appeared at the door of the room. "All set," he said. "Come up the back way."

"Anyone see you?"

148

Hardtack grinned as he helped himself to a drink. "Not when I don't want to be seen."

Rowan followed the old man down the back stairs, across the alleyway and through a littered lot to dark Yucca Street.

Hardtack turned left down the street and walked to Fourth Street. He held Rowan back and scouted toward Bonanza. They crossed the street swiftly. This end of town was dark in comparison to the area farther east between Second and Yucca.

Hardtack stopped at the edge of the yawning stope into which Rowan had nearly fallen when he had first come to town. "Here we are," he said.

"You damned fool! The heading is up the hill."

"You think I don't know, you damned jackass? They think we'll enter the mine up there."

"So?"

Hardtack spat into the stope. "You can get into the mine just as easy from here, sonny."

Rowan looked dubiously down into the dark hole. "Let's go up to the heading," he suggested.

Hardtack gripped Rowan with a skinny claw. "Who in hell's name do you think will be up there waiting for us amongst that rusty scrap iron? I tell yuh, I can get into the main drifts through here. You coming or do I go alone?"

Rowan looked up the hill toward the gaunt structures etched against the dark sky. "All right," he said. "I should know better – but go ahead."

Hardtack worked his way down the slope, as happy as a woodchuck returning to his hole. "All right!" he called, "slide toward me. I'll ketch yuh."

Rowan glanced up and down the deserted street, then slid down the slope in a rattle of gravel. Just when he was getting ready to curse Hardtack, the old man gripped him with surprising strength and jerked him into a pitch-black hole. The gravel continued to fall, pattering far below. There was the scratch of a match, and Rowan saw the bearded face of the old man as he lit a lantern. Hardtack indicated a pair of shovels and picks, another lantern, coils of rope, candles and a packet of food. They picked up the gear. Hardtack led the way along the sagging drift which had ended at the collapsed stope.

Their feet echoed hollowly as they passed side drifts. Now and then Rowan looked up to see sagging roof props. They clambered over heaps of fallen earth and skirted holes in the uneven floor. Rowan had checked the time of their entry by his repeater watch. It had been a little after nine P.M.

Hardtack led the way with the sureness of a mole penetrating his own burrows. In half an hour Rowan was lost. If anything happened to the old man he would be down there until he died. Now and then Hardtack stopped at a cross drift and then, with a grunt, would continue on. Twice he took side tunnels and forged on. At the end of an hour and a half Hardtack stopped and sat down on a pile of props. "Set," he said.

Rowan sat down and shoved back his hat. "You sure you know where you are?"

"If I don't, I been slipping the last few years."

"You haven't been down here for years."

Hardtack took out a bottle. "Yeah? Don't be too sure, sonny."

"What do you mean by that?"

Hardtack drank deeply and passed the bottle to Rowan. The old man wiped his mouth on a dirty sleeve. "Yuh think I never looked for that bullion before? I been all through this mess. One time I got in a brawl in the Barrel House and cut a man up. Lacey was hot on my trail. I grabbed some food and hid down here a week until the mess blew over. Kinda damp at times, but it was a helluva lot better than sitting in the *calabozo*."

Rowan sat there, eying the old man. Far ahead he heard the drip of water. There was a distant fall of earth. A cold wind searched through the tunnel, and Rowan shivered a little. He pulled at the bottle twice.

"Come on," said Hardtack. He picked up his gear and plunged into the darkness, his lantern casting alternate pools of light and banks of shadow as he went on, at times outlining his spare figure. It reminded Rowan of a picture he had seen a Mex prisoner draw on a cell wall at Yuma – the gaunt figure of Father Time, complete with scythe and lantern. The pick Hardtack carried reminded Rowan of the scythe.

"Watch your step," the old man called back. He stopped and held up his lantern. A hole gaped in the tunnel floor. Hardtack ran forward and jumped, landing on his haunches on the far side and balancing precariously, only to fall forward on his face. Something struck the side of the pit. A moment later there was a splash far below. "God damn!" said Hardtack. "Dropped my damned Colt."

"Look out," said Rowan. He sprinted forward and jumped the gap easily. He reached in his pocket and gave Hardtack his double-barreled derringer.

Hardtack pocketed the deadly little weapon. He glanced down the hole.

"Sam Corbett won't like that," he said.

"Why?"

Hardtack grinned. "I pinched it from the jail office when he released me today."

"Damned old reprobate," said Rowan.

"Yeah, ain't I though?" Hardtack went on. "Guess one of the tommyknockers is on our trail," he said.

"Tommyknockers?"

The old man glanced back at Rowan. "Yeah. The 'little people' of the mines. They carry off tools and play pranks. The Germans call them *kobolds*. The Mexicans call them *duendes*. I guess tommyknocker is English."

"So?"

"They can play hell down here. Wait!" Hardtack stopped so quickly that Rowan had his Colt out and cocked before the old man waved a hand. "Ain't nothing. Watch!" Hardtack took out a piece of bread and meat and placed it on a heap of earth. He turned. "Leave 'em some food," he whispered, "then they leave you alone – sometimes."

The old man's face looked like a satyr's as he leered at Rowan. Then he was off on his swift way. He raised his voice in a cracked baritone:

153

"I'm a hardrock miner an' I ain't afeard of
   ghosts,
But my neck hair bristles like a porcupine's
   quills
An' I knock my knuckles on the drift-
   set posts
When the tommyknockers hammer on the
   caps an' sills
An' raise hallelujah with my pick an'
   drills."

Rowan shook his head. He was beginning to
wonder about old Horatio Christie, pride of
Crib Row.

Hardtack turned. "Accidents always
happen in threes," he said mysteriously.
"Losing the gun was number one."

"Damn you. You're sandpapering my
nerves now."

"Hell of a miner you woulda made."

"You'd never have got me to work beside
you, you damned old vinegarroon!"

"Sho? This is the gratitude I get."

"If you don't shut up I'll find Angie and tell
her you made a new strike."

"God forbid! I'll shut up."

Half an hour later they met their first
serious earth fall, blocking the tunnel clear
to the roof. Rowan did the work, sweating

and cursing in the confined area until he cut through to the other side. Hardtack slid through the hole and sniffed the air. "All right," he said. "Fresh as a daisy."

"Where are we now, Horatio?"

"I calculate we'll hit one of the main drifts soon. Must be damned near the mine heading by now."

It was midnight when Hardtack called a halt. They sat in the dim pool of lantern light, gnawing on thick beef sandwiches. The lantern was burning low. Hardtack looked at it and spat to one side. "Angie's out with another man," he said.

"How do you know?"

Hardtack spat out a piece of gristle. "Lamp is burning low."

"Good God!"

Hardtack shook his head. "Lotsa jokin' about that in a mine, but I seen tough hardrock boys quit work in the middle of a shift and go home just to make sure."

"You're a regular encyclopedia of mining lore, aren't you?" jeered Rowan.

"I don't know what a damned syclepedia is, sonny. But I know a lot about mines."

Rowan looked at his repeater watch. "Midnight," he said.

"Bad time. We'll rest awhile."

"You worn out already?"

Hardtack sagged back against the wall and took a pull from his bottle. "No. But if you had any sense you wouldn't move around too much in a mine at midnight. Accidents like midnight to happen."

Rowan rubbed his jaw. He looked at the solid wall of darkness hemming them in and then reached for the bottle.

CHAPTER TWELVE

It was impossible for Rowan to get Hardtack to move on again until it was half past twelve. Shortly after they started on, Hardtack stepped from the drift into a larger tunnel. "Main drift," he said over his shoulder. "Most of the levels below here are full of water." He set off at a rapid pace away from the mine heading.

It was past one o'clock when Hardtack stopped again. He turned and looked intently past Rowan. Rowan turned also. "What is it?" he whispered.

"Thought I heard somethin'," said Hardtack.

They stood there with the drip, drip, drip of water sounding far below them in an open shaft. Rowan shrugged impatiently. "Come on," he said.

Hardtack shook his head. "No. I heard something."

Rowan listened. Then he heard a low, muttering noise. A chill went up his back. Voices. He looked at Hardtack. The old man scratched in his ragged beard. "You hear it now?" he whispered hoarsely.

Rowan started. Far down the drift he saw a flash of yellow light. Behind Hardtack was a side drift. He shoved the old man toward it. They doused their lanterns, and Rowan drew his Colt and cocked it. The noise grew louder and they could distinguish individual voices. Boots squelched in the pools of water which dotted the drift floor. Rowan and Hardtack stepped behind props and flattened themselves against the damp walls.

The flicker of a lantern showed at the mouth of the side drift. "This is a damned fool trip," growled a familiar voice, that of Dan Lacey. "We'll fall into an open shaft. They ain't down here, Walt."

The lantern light flooded the drift for a moment as the men went past. Rowan saw the hard, intent face of Durango. The light passed on.

"They're in here, dammit," said Walt Sharpe. "Where else would they be?"

The footsteps squelched on.

Hardtack moved. "They musta got by Arch Lang," he whispered.

Rowan cursed. He walked to the main drift and looked down it. The three men moved slowly along in the pool of light. Hardtack shifted. Suddenly he tripped and fell. Rowan whirled. "Damn it!" he hissed. "Be quiet!"

Silence followed. The drip of water sounded hollowly from far below. "Rowan!" said Hardtack, "bring a light."

"You loco?"

"Bring a light!"

Rowan turned and felt his way to Hardtack. He scratched a lucifer against his belt buckle. In the brief flare of light he saw Hardtack on his knees beside a pile of something. The old man looked up. "Here's your damned silver!" he said. "Every blessed bar of it!"

Rowan dropped to his knees and cursed as the match burned his fingers. He lit another one. The bars were piled beneath a moldy tarp, which Hardtack had thrown back. Rowan looked closely at one of them. It was stamped with the company mark. Hardtack stood up. His eyes glittered in the flare of the match. "By God," he said. "Fifty thousand!"

Rowan blew out the match and listened. There was no sound from up the main drift. "We'll wait here until they leave," he said.

"Pass me the bottle then."

The cork popped out and Rowan heard the gurgle as the old man took a hooker. The fumes of whisky drifted to him. Rowan turned. The noise had come again.

"Rowan," quavered Hardtack.

"Shut up. They're coming back."

"Give me a light, for the love of God!"

Something in the old man's tone caused Rowan to light a match. Hardtack was standing behind the pile of bullion, looking down. Rowan skirted the ingots. Before the match flickered out he saw something lying on the damp floor – a grinning skull, a bony form dressed in rags. It was the rotten cowhide vest that burned into his mind. Larry Farber had worn such a vest the night he had ridden from Silver Rock as guard for the bullion.

Footsteps squelched in the mud. Hardtack shifted, and there was a clattering noise. He had knocked over a shovel.

"You hear that?" called Durango.

"They're back there, I'll bet!" said Lacey. "In that side drift we passed!"

Rowan knelt behind the ingots. The boots thudded, coming closer. The lantern light showed again. Then there was silence. Rowan rested his right arm on the ingots, aiming his Colt toward the mouth of the side drift.

"You're hearing things," said Sharpe.

"Damned if I am," said Lacey.

"Nothing there," said Walt.

"Go in there then!"

"You heard the noise. *You* go in. There's nothing there."

"I'll show you!"

Feet squelched in the mud. A head poked around the side of the entrance. Rowan did not move. Suddenly Lacey ran past the drift entrance. Rowan waited. Minutes drifted past.

"Let's get out of here," said Sharpe. "Lacey, you damned fool! There ain't nothing in there."

"Well, I'm going to look."

Lacey appeared in the lamplight, holding his Colt. He walked into the drift, stepped behind a prop and thrust out an arm. There was the sharp double click of a cocking weapon. Rowan fired, and Lacey cursed. Smoke flowed out of the drift. Lacey fired three shots straight into the drift. Hardtack grunted. Rowan jumped to his feet, stepped behind a prop and fired. Lacey came out from behind his prop, turned slowly and fell face down into the thin layer of mud on the drift floor.

Hardtack groaned, and Rowan knelt beside him. "Got me through the left shoulder," whispered Hardtack. Rowan crawled back into the drift and lit a match. The way was partially blocked by a fall. It would take time to dig through and get Hardtack to safety. Rowan cursed. Suddenly he turned. Two figures showed as shadows on the far wall of the main drift.

"You think he got him?" asked Durango.

"Hell yes! Lacey don't miss."

"Yeah? *Then where's Lacey?*"

Sharpe cursed. "I'll show you." The shadow fell across the drift mouth, and the familiar figure of Walt Sharpe appeared. The light glittered on the nickel-plated Colt in his hand. Rowan fired twice. The man staggered back, fired once, then fell back out of sight.

Rowan eased behind a pit prop. One left, the most dangerous of the three. Durango, of the cold, light blue eyes. The knifer. Minutes dragged past. There was a faint noise at the front of the drift. Suddenly an arm, holding the lantern, appeared. The arm swung the lantern hard. It smashed against the pile of ingots. Rowan leaped out to clear the flaming fluid, dropping his Colt. A pistol stabbed red flame into the tunnel, and the report boomed like a cannon. Rowan fell back over the pile of bullion. It was pitch dark. Rowan felt through Hardtack's clothing. "Where's the derringer?" he whispered.

"Damned ... if ... I know," said Hardtack.

Rowan gripped a shovel.

A low laugh sounded at the front of the drift. "You there, Emmett?" It was Durango.

There was the noise of a lantern cylinder being slid up, the flare of a match and then the steady glow of a lantern. The light came from the side of the drift. Durango stepped into the light. "Shoot, you bastard," he said. A Colt was held ready in his hand.

Rowan gripped Hardtack to keep him quiet. Durango stepped out of sight. "Got you!" he said. He laughed. "Maybe you're wounded, Emmett. I saw your Colt on the floor. Maybe you're helpless back there."

The inhuman laugh came again. The light moved, and Durango appeared, holding the lantern. Rowan had to give the killer credit. It took animal courage to come into that silent drift. Durango moved behind a thick prop. He waited. "I'm coming in, Rowan," he said. "You would have fired by now."

Rowan shifted and gripped the shovel. Durango stepped into the drift and came forward slowly. He placed the lantern on a natural shelf at the side of the drift. He holstered his Colt and drew his knife, testing the edge on his thumb. Then he moved close to the pile of ingots.

Rowan came up over the bullion, swinging hard with the shovel. Durango crouched beneath the sweep of the shovel and laughed. He moved in closer. Rowan struck hard. The shovel hit a prop, forcing Rowan to drop it, Durango darted in and struck with the knife. The tip ripped through Rowan's coat and cut the skin of his belly. Blood trickled down his body.

Durango came in. Rowan stooped for the shovel and then leaped back as the knife slashed his neck. He backed to a prop, looking about for a weapon.

Durango laughed thinly. Suddenly he moved, whipping the knife hard in a side-arm throw. The blade flashed and struck hard, pinning Rowan's left coat sleeve to the prop. Stinging pain swept through his bicep, where the skin had been pinned to the prop. Blood flowed down his arm. Rowan gripped the knife and tried to free it, but the blade was fast in the damp wood.

Durango drew his Colt and cocked it. He eyed Rowan. "Where do you want it? Belly or head?"

A gun spat flame from the mouth of the side drift. Durango staggered and dropped the Colt. His mouth opened wide as though to speak, and then he pitched forward across the pile of bullion. Smoke spread through the drift. A man walked into the drift with ready Colt. Rowan could have yelled for joy as he saw the lean face of Archer Lang.

The gambler hooked a boot toe beneath Durango and rolled him from the pile. He looked up at Rowan. "Just in time, eh, *amigo?*"

Lang pulled the knife free and threw it out of the drift. "You've had a time down here, Rowan."

Rowan knelt beside Hardtack and spoke over his shoulder. "Bring that lantern."

Lang brought the lantern and held it high while Rowan ripped Hardtack's shirt away from the wound. He bound it swiftly with a bandanna, after dousing it with whisky. He stood up and gripped Archer by the shoulder. "He'll be all right. There's the silver, Arch."

Lang looked down at it. "Fifty thousand!" he said. "Enough for a man to get by if he knows where to place it."

"Yeah. *I* know where to place it, Arch." Rowan pointed at the skeleton on the floor at the rear of the bullion. "Larry Farber," he said. "There's a mystery here that has to be unraveled."

Lang lit a cigar. He studied the skeleton. "Yeah. Cigar, Rowan?"

Rowan nodded. Lang reached inside his coat. The white of a bandage showed at the base of his neck. Rowan looked quickly at it. "Where'd you get that, Arch?" he asked.

Lang's dark eyes held Rowan's. "From you."

"*You loco?*

Lang shook his head. "The night Cassie was shot. You damned near got me, Rowan."

Rowan stared incredulously. "I don't understand."

Lang kicked Rowan's Colt from beneath his feet and raised his own weapon. "I shot Cassie Whitlow, Rowan. She was about to warn you about me."

Rowan felt cold sweat break out beneath his armpits. He stared at the gambler. Far below them he heard the steady drip, drip, drip of water.

CHAPTER THIRTEEN

Archer Lang leaned against a pit prop and puffed at his cigar. Rowan sat down on the pile of bullion and looked at the man he had thought was his friend. Hardtack groaned softly. Rowan looked at the old man. "We've got to get him out of here, "he said.

Lang shook his head. "Let him stay! We've

got work to do getting this bullion out of here."

"You can't leave him here in this damp!"

Lang spat. "He's lived too long already."

"You cold-gutted shark!"

Archer Lang laughed. "I've been called worse than that."

Rowan looked at the shovel lying against the wall.

"Don't try it, Rowan," warned Lang. He eyed the pile of silver. "It was a damned long wait to get my hands on that," he said.

"You were in this from the start then?"

Lang nodded. "I talked Larry into the deal. You remember I worked for the mining company at the time? A *trusted* employee. Making forty dollars a week when the bosses were taking thousands a day out of this hole. Larry was like me. Tired of working for pennies. I planned the whole thing. It was me who waited in the brush along the creek road. I killed Mike and thought I had taken care of you."

Rowan touched the faint line of scar which cut along the side of his head.

Lang relit his cigar, watching Rowan keenly. "I had already picketed some mules in the brush. Larry and I worked fast, taking the silver to that old drift you and Hardtack

166

found. Larry and I had opened it up the week before the robbery. In those days most of the drifts over this way had already been abandoned but were still in good shape. Larry took the mules right into the tunnels. We worked like fiends that night."

Rowan spat. The simile was good.

"While the silver was being stored away by Larry, I kept guard in the wash. It was almost dawn when he came out of the drift. I went down into the drift to see where the silver was stored. Larry shot at me. I fired back, wounding him. He disappeared down the drift. I went after him but he kept firing. I hid in the brush outside for hours and then went into the drift. There was no sign of Larry. He was somewhere in here, wounded or dead, with fifty thousand dollars in silver cached in a place I had no knowledge of."

Rowan shrugged. "The biter got bit," he said wryly.

Lang looked quickly at him. "I had to go back to town to report for work, as it would look too suspicious for me to be missing. It was then I learned that you were still alive. I didn't dare look for the bullion as long as there was so much excitement about the trial." Lang laughed grimly. "Even after you were in Yuma it didn't make a damned bit of difference. I prowled through drift after drift trying to find the silver, but it was no use. Years went by and the mines flooded. When you returned I knew you were determined to find that silver. I figured I'd keep an eye on you, helping you, hoping somehow you'd blunder on to the lost cache." Lang laughed. He kicked the pile of ingots.

"It was you who killed Ellis, then?"

"Keno! He was getting too damned curious."

"What about Darby?"

Lang spat. "Amos always was suspicious of me. The card argument was a good excuse to get rid of him."

"Yet you let him draw first."

Lang nodded. "I had to make it *look* good," he said coldly. He relit his cigar. "The one big flaw was Cassie. She knew everything. I didn't figure on her still liking you as much as she did. Evidently she thought I'd never cut her in on the bullion. I had to keep her mouth shut."

Rowan felt a sour taste in the back of his mouth. He felt as though he was in the company of a copperhead. "Now what?" he asked quietly.

"We'll get some of this out of here."

Rowan stood up. "Then what?"

Lang smiled. "We'll talk about that later."

Rowan bent over Hardtack. "You all right, oldtimer?" he asked.

Hardtack opened his eyes. "I told yuh accidents always happen by threes," he said.

Lang jerked his Colt. "Get up, Rowan," he said. "Take that rope and some of that canvas. Make a sling. You're going to be my burro tonight."

"You bastard," said Rowan.

Rowan got Durango's knife and cut some of the canvas into pieces, tying them in sling form with the pieces of rope. He placed some of the ingots in them and stood up, eying the cold-eyed gambler. "Well?"

"Back to the heading."

Rowan shrugged.

"What's the matter?"

"Nothing."

Lang nodded. "Maybe you've got someone waiting back there? Is that it?"

Rowan spat. *"You're* doing all the thinking."

Lang picked up the lantern and a shovel. "We'll go out the other way."

Rowan shifted his load. "Lead on, Macduff," he said.

The gambler glanced nervously at Rowan. "I hate these damned holes in the ground," he said.

"You shouldn't. It's the natural place for a snake."

For a moment fine lines etched themselves at the corners of Lang's mouth. "Go on," he said thinly. "Joke all you want, Rowan. I'll have the *last* laugh."

Rowan slogged on. It was hard going on the slick floor. Now and then they clambered over heaps of fallen earth. The farther along they went, the worse the going became, until at last they faced a fall that filled the tunnel. Lang threw the shovel on the floor. "Dig," he said.

Rowan lowered the sling and picked up the shovel. He attacked the pile of earth. Lang leaned against a pit prop. "You damned near got away with it, Rowan," he said.

"What do you mean?"

"Going in through the old stope."

"It was Hardtack's idea."

Lang nodded. "I was up at the pit head when Sharpe, Lacey and Durango came up there looking for you. I knew damned well something had gone wrong. I followed them. Almost thought they had you."

Rowan spat and worked at the loose earth. Sweat ran down his body and stung his knife cuts. Twice he glanced back to see if he could get a swing at Lang with the shovel, but the gambler's cold eyes warned him.

Rowan felt the shovel break through, and a draft met his face. There was a faint odor of mesquite about it. "Hand me the light," he said.

Lang passed the light up to Rowan. He thrust it through the hole. Just beyond the earth fall was a yawning pit. Then he knew where he was – in the drift that he and Hardtack had broken into. He passed the lantern back and slid down the earth pile to pick up the ingot sling.

"Look all right?" asked Lang.

"Just more tunnel," said Rowan quietly.

"You go first."

Rowan shrugged. He worked his way through the hole and slid down the earth pile. The pit was about ten feet behind him. Lang pushed the lantern through the hole and thrust his arm, holding the Colt, ahead of him. He worked his way through and reached for the lantern. Rowan slipped out of the sling and dived for the gambler. Lang cursed and slashed at Rowan with the gun barrel. Rowan gripped the gun wrist and forced it high, driving in a solid punch to Lang's lean gut.

Lang grunted. Rowan pulled the gun arm down hard and raised his left knee, smashing Lang's hand on the kneecap. Lang dropped the Colt with a curse. Rowan rushed the tall man back against the damp drift wall. Lang brought up a knee into Rowan's groin, and Rowan doubled in agony. Lang smashed his joined hands down on the back of Rowan's neck. Rowan fell flat and rolled over. Lang reached for the Colt, but Rowan kicked hard. The Colt slithered over the floor, and a moment later there was a distant splash.

Lang spat. He snatched up the shovel and rushed at Rowan. Rowan hooked his left foot behind Lang's right ankle and kicked hard at the inside of the gambler's right knee. Lang went backwards and hit hard. Then Rowan was on him like a tiger. Lang's hands gripped Rowan's throat. They rolled over against the wall. Rowan broke free and gripped the tall man by the front of his coat. He drove in short, smashing blows to the face, battering Lang's head back against a prop. Lang's nails clawed Rowan's face, feeling for the eyes. Blood ran down Rowan's face, and then he broke free. Lang got up and slashed Rowan across the nose with his open hand. Tears blinded him. His foot hit the lantern, shattering it. Darkness enveloped them.

Rowan lay still, trying to control his harsh breathing. He heard Lang move. "I've got my derringer," panted Lang. "Give up, Rowan. I'll give you a fair shake."

Rowan did not answer.

"I'll split with you, Rowan. We were always friends!"

Rowan lay flat, staring into the darkness. Lang was but a few feet from the pit.

"You hear me, Rowan?"

The derringer spat flame. The slug hit a prop. In the quick flash Rowan saw the gambler's battered face. Then darkness again. Rowan's hand closed on one of the ingots that had slipped from the sling. Lang had one more shot.

Minutes ticked past. Lang shifted. "I'll give you three to give up, Rowan," he said. "Then I shoot."

Rowan was silent. He shifted to free his throwing arm.

"One!" counted Lang. "Two! *Three!*"

As the gun flashed, Rowan threw the ingot with all his strength. It caught the gambler in the face. Lang screamed like a stricken horse. There was a rattle of loose earth in the pitch darkness and then another long-drawn scream, followed by a splash far below. Earth trickled down, pattering on the surface of the water.

Rowan lay flat on the cold mud of the drift floor. There was a sour bile taste in the back of his throat. He sat up and wiped his face. He fumbled for matches, lighting one of the candles he had slipped into his coat pocket. He walked to the edge of the pit and looked down. There was nothing but shadow below him. He turned, clambered up the earth fall and walked slowly back to Hardtack.

The old man lifted his head as Rowan came into the drift. "For God's sake!" he said. "A ghost!"

Rowan spat. "You damned idiot!" he said. "You ever see a ghost as battered and bleeding as I am?"

Hardtack eased himself up. "Where's Lang?"

Rowan pointed down. "Fell in a pit, Hardtack."

"With your help."

"Yeah." Rowan unstoppered the bottle and handed it to Hardtack. He took a drink himself. "Can you walk?"

"Hell yes. A little wobbly, maybe, but I can make it."

Rowan helped him to his feet. He looked at the pile of silver. In the light of the candle it seemed to have a rosy glow. Blood, thought Rowan. The blood that had been shed over it. "Come on, Horatio," he said. "I'll never get out of this damned suburb of hell without you."

"You leaving the silver?"

"It's safe enough," said Rowan.

Hardtack looked at the three bodies sprawled in the much of the floor. "Yeah. With three *patrons*."

"What do you mean?"

Hardtack waved his good hand. "The old Spanish miners always left a dead man behind so's his ghost could guard the bullion. We're leavin' three. Let's go, *amigo*."

They trudged wearily down the tunnel. Tired and battered as Rowan was, he felt as though the weight of ten long years had been lifted from his shoulders.

They climbed the ladders in the pit heading. Hardtack cursed at every rung. Gray dawn light flooded down on them as they reached the level below the surface. "Someone's coming!" a man yelled. Rowan reached the top and looked into the anxious face of Ellen Farber. Jim Bond, holding a lantern and dressed in rough clothing, stood beside her. A dozen townsmen were clustered behind them. Hardtack climbed up beside Rowan and stared at the group.

Bond gripped Rowan's hand. "We were coming after you," he said.

Rowan looked at the men. "The stolen bullion is safe down there," he said.

"What about the others who went down there?"

Hardtack drew his hand across his throat in a swift gesture.

Ellen came close to Rowan and gently touched his battered face. "Somehow I knew you'd come back," she said quietly.

Bond looked about at the men. "We might as well go and get breakfast." He grinned at Rowan. "I want an exclusive on this story, Rowan."

Rowan smiled. "I won't give it to another paper in Silver Rock," he promised.

They walked slowly down the hill in the gray light of dawn. In the east there was a tint of rose and gold as the sun came up behind the distant mountains.

Jim Bond placed an arm about Rowan's shoulders. "There's a ten-thousand-dollar reward posted for the apprehension of the men who stole the silver, and for its recovery, as well as for the murderer, or murderers, who killed Mike Ganoe."

Rowan glanced at the newspaperman. "It was Archer Lang," he said. There was an unspoken message in his eyes.

Bond flushed and glanced at Ellen. "I see. Anyway, it's yours, Rowan."

Rowan glanced back at Hardtack. "Can you use five thousand dollars, Hardtack?"

"Hell yes," the old man called.

One of the men turned to look at Hardtack.

"Say, Hardtack," he said. "There's a lady come in late last night. Looked all over town for you."

Hardtack paled. He looked at Rowan.

"Is her name Angie?" asked Rowan.

"Yeh. That's it! Angie!"

Hardtack turned and started back up the slope.

"Where are you going?" called Jim Bond.

"Back to the mine!" yelled Hardtack over his shoulder. "This is *one* strike I'm going to keep for myself! Let me know when she's gone!"

The sun tipped the eastern mountains as they reached the center of town. Rowan put his arm about Ellen. "It isn't a bad town, Ellen," he said. "Especially now – fresh and bright in the morning sun."

"I've always liked it. It's had its share of trouble. Maybe it's on the right trail at last."

Rowan nodded as he watched the sun flood the eastern desert with clear light, outlining the distant peaks. Somewhere a lark bugled clearly. He was on the right trail at last. The trail of darkness had ended, far below the earth beneath their feet.